THE GIRL WITH THE WICKER BASKET

or

THE IRISH EGGMAN

A TALE OF HARDSHIP, LOVE AND THE QUEST FOR A BETTER LIFE IN NINETEENTH CENTURY IRELAND

James T Maloney

Chapter 1

The Boreen

It was the boreen's[1] fault; some of the holes in the track were deeper than your ankle and brim full with bog brown water.

It was the boreen's fault that the donkey-cart lurched into one of the deeper holes that was impossible to avoid when hidden by the overnight rain.

It was the boreen's fault the backboard dropped open, allowing two of the egg boxes to slide off the cart.

Perhaps it was Tom's fault for hurrying to reach a better road before the frowning rain clouds looking down on his progress dispensed their watery burden again, turning the pot-holed track into a millrace. The centre of the track was relatively even, with a sparse growth of grass making it not too hazardous for the donkey, the danger was when the cart swayed as its wheels discovered the hidden water filed potholes.

Looking South-west, beyond the scurrying grey clouds Tom could see pale blue fingers of sunlight grasping the barren peak of Croagh Patrick the revered holy mountain, as if trying to examine what lay beneath.

The cart was now more than half way along the deeply rutted boreen between the Walsh farm and the better-maintained road that led to nearby Ballingar. A track that young Tom Walsh knew like the back of his hand, almost every day for the last twenty years he travelled along it. He knew where the worst of the hazards were in the poorly maintained track, by noting a particular stunted tree, fence post, or the shape of a boulder in the low stone walls on either side of the track. Today he wasn't concentrating on the task in hand, his mind was elsewhere.

Yet there was hope of a brighter day ahead.

---

[1]   Boreen, a narrow unpaved rural road.

Chapter 2

The Boreen 2

Tom had been up early, for today is the day he makes the twice weekly
journey to Westport, delivering the eggs he had collected during the week
to the exporter at Westport Quay. After a quick wash at the old stone glazed
sink, ever hungry Tom, consumed the remains of a loaf with each slice
coated with a copious layer of freshly churned butter, before quickly sorting
and packing the last of the eggs collected the previous two days.

Tom's thoughts were anywhere but on the task in hand, that probably
accounted for the boxes not being tied as securely as they should have. He
was having difficulty concentrating and it wasn't all down to the late night
drinking in Campbell's bar.
Steering the cart slowly around the deepest holes in the road should have
been his main preoccupation, today was different; he had other things on
his mind.

Looking to his left in one of the many fields enclosed by low dry stone
walls that blanket the side of the hill, Tom's neighbour Shamus Griffin was
calling in his two brown and white cows, their udders swollen to bursting
ready for milking in the simple shelter that serves as a shippon. Shamus
acknowledged Tom with a casual wave of his hazel walking stick before
turning to open the rickety wooden gate which had to be lifted due to it's
worn hinges.

To his right, in the fields still imprinted with the shadow of last year's
lazy-beds, other early rising cottiers were occupied preparing the soil for
the first early crop of potatoes.

After stopping to carefully re-pack and rope down the boxes Tom
gingerly continued on his way, trying to avoid the worst of the humps and
hollows that made the cart sway like his father after a night drinking the
hard stuff. Luckily for Tom his father insisted on packing the eggs in sturdy
wooden cases with ample layers of dry straw protecting the fragile goods,
which meant that less than a dozen eggs were ruined.

Tom was on his weekly run from the Townland of Knockaun to Westport
Quay, taking eggs to be exported to England to feed the populous moving

from the rural villages to the crowded streets and terraces of the ever growing industrial cities.

The rest of the week Tom was mainly occupied collecting fresh eggs from small farms around Knockaun and packing them ready for transporting to the port. He preferred it to other tasks around the farm, like the backbreaking drudgery of preparing the fields for the next crop of potatoes, or cutting, loading and stacking turf from the nearby bog.

Tom's father Joseph Walsh encouraged his children to leave home, realising the small farm could never sustain all of his brood.

Ten years earlier Tom's uncle, out of desperate necessity followed the well-trodden path of Irish migrants to Wolverhampton in the heart of industrial England. He found lodging with an Irish family who helped him find work in the local Iron Works. On returning to the farm for a family wedding, he was quick to tell of factories like the iron works and coal mines where finding employment was easy. Addressing ears that had never ventured beyond the shores of Erin and eager for news from across the sea he told them.

'They're crying out for labour.' Usually omitting to tell of the overcrowded streets and tenements of every industrialised metropolis in England as farm labourer's leave the land and flock to the factories to feed the ravenous wheels of industry.

Straight talking Joe Walsh saw for himself the opportunities in England when he travelled there to work as a 'harvest man'. His business acumen meant that he was well regarded among the local cottiers,[2] which prompted them to ask him to act as Ganger organising 'harvest men'[3] to make the annual journey to England to work on farms helping to 'bring in' the ripened corn.

Tom had often thought about leaving home to work in England; at night around the dinner table his father would say, 'your mother makes you too comfortable here Thomas, Mick and I can manage the farm, try it for a year, you can always come home.' Tom would just shrug his shoulders and say,

'One day da, one day.'

A bright blue sky slowly replaced the patchwork of dark clouds fulfilling the promise of better weather and now the cart was on a more even road. Still, Tom found it hard to concentrate on the task in hand, his thoughts

2
3

drifting, thinking about past times, especially the events of the last three weeks. What the day will bring?

Today is different Tom had other things on his mind.

---

[2]   *Cottier, an Irish peasant holding land by cottier tenure.*
[3]   *Harvest Men are seasonal Irish workers that travel to England and Scotland in the 19th and 20th century, providing extra labour at harvest time, sleeping in barns or other temporary accommodation provided by the farmer.*

Chapter 3

Thomas Walsh and his siblings

Born in the year eighteen fifty-seven, Thomas Walsh a stocky twenty-two years old with dark hair and flashing intelligent brown eyes the youngest of Joseph and Honor Walsh's six children (four boys, Michael, Patrick, Joseph and Thomas, and two girls, Bridget and Maria).

Thomas was born at a time when Ireland was still recovering from the disaster that the Irish call 'The Great Hunger'. A disaster the Government in England called 'The Irish Potato Famine'.

The room where Thomas first saw the light of day was in a typical grass thatched Irish cottage. A cottage that is like most of the others in Knockaun except that it is longer, and has more outbuildings indicating the prosperity of the occupants.

Tom's eldest brother Michael...tall and ruddy faced with red hair and a temperament to match...is expected to inherit the farm, egg and haulage business and is running it all with the guidance of his ageing father Joseph. Like his maternal grandfather, Michael is easily politically motivated, arguing and banging his fist on the table during heated debates about any injustice inflicted by the ruling classes. His mother sympathises with him, remembering her grandfather, a local hero and legend, remembered by the community as one of those hanged at Castlebar for joining the French troops as they marched through the town in seventeen ninety eight. She often told to her boys when they were growing up to fight for justice but to tread carefully saying, 'remember your great grandfather.'

Tom's brother Patrick said farewell to Mayo and the shores of Ireland three years earlier and is in New York working the docks according to the solitary letter to reach home.

Joseph Walsh crossed the Irish Sea to England to see for himself whether life really is better on the other side of the water, found work labouring in a Manchester cotton mill.

Bridget, the eldest of the two girls...to the disappointment of her father...is married to an Englishman and has two children is also living in Manchester and working in a cotton mill.

Maria Walsh is the baby of the family. Eighteen years old, fair of face complemented by attractive freckles...which she hates... and crowned by light brown hair, the youngest of the girls and still at home waiting her turn to leave the nest.

Chapter 4

The Walsh Farm

The Walsh farm is situated in the west of Ireland on a windswept East Mayo hillside, where four small hamlets make up the townland of Knockaun. The residents call themselves farmers; at least that is what the government Inspectors put on their forms.

Farms on the Western Seaboard of Ireland usually follow the same pattern; and the Walsh farm is no exception; a three room stone cabin...now extended...roofed with a thatch of grass. Outside is an open ended shed, mainly used for storing turf, (the free fuel extracted from the bog half a mile away) next to a stone barn with a lean-to shelter, which serves as an open stable to shelter the horses, and donkeys. Away from the house is a stone built pig sty, housing a breeding sow with a litter of nine piglets and a grumpy bore in the next pen. More recent additions are rows of chicken coops producing eggs for export as well as an extra source of food.

Within a few months of Tom's father Joe Walsh taking over the farm he realised the land was poor and undernourished. The rubble-ridden soil could just about yield a miserable harvest of oats, or potatoes. The soil had become sour in need of feeding to enable it to produce a decent crop. To make matters worse most of the fields were littered with rocky outcrops, like grey icebergs in a brown sea.

One farmer when asked how much land he had replied, 'I have a bit of land and a rock, then another bit of land, and another rock'.

Joe Walsh set about making the land more productive and realising that the farm could never support a large family. After living through the 'famine years' he encouraged Tom and his brothers to become self-sufficient vowing that his family would never again go hungry.

The land farmed by Tom's grandfather had been divided forty years earlier when Tom's father Joe married, giving Joe...the eldest son...eight and a half acres.

Joe could see all around him that the old tradition of repeatedly dividing the land between sons, had compounded the wretchedness of the 'famine years.' and decided that this tradition would have to end, at least it would

11

end in his family.

During one of his visits to the cattle market at Ballingar, Joe made the acquaintance of farmers from as far afield as Sligo and Enniskillen. After business was concluded it was usual to retire to the nearest bar where over a few jars of ale Joe heard one of the farmers from Inniskillen relate how he was able to supplement his income by carting goods to and from the docks in Sligo.

Three months later Joe had raised enough cash to buy a draught horse and an old four wheel cart and soon had enough work to start hauling goods to and from Westport Quay and Sligo docks.

Joe like most of the small farmers in rural Ireland kept fowl and pigs, not only to feed their families but also to add to their meagre income. Realising this could be another means of income Joe gradually increased his stock of laying hens until he established himself as a producer and later a buyer of eggs. Encouraged by the success of the egg business he continued building more hen houses and chicken runs on the less productive land close to the house doubling, then trebling the number of laying hens on his farm, and encouraged his neighbours to do the same, telling them that he will buy all the eggs they produce to sell on to be exported to England.

Joe's youngest son Tom was the only member of his family to attend the recently opened National School...Joe was keen for him to be educated unlike his other sons. Michael, the eldest, worked on the farm every day from the age of seven.

From an early age after school and during the annual summer school holiday Tom joined his brother Michael on the twice-weekly egg collecting round, calling at local farms buying eggs for cash or sometimes in barter for produce. Back at the farm the eggs were carefully sorted and packed in straw lined crates before being carted to the docks at Westport or Sligo to be shipped to England.

Thus the business of Joseph Walsh and Sons Farmer, dealer in Eggs and Carter of goods were established.

Chapter 5

The Wicker Basket

Three Weeks earlier.
The unspoiled view of Clew Bay and Clare Island with its attendant drumlins[4] scattered across the bay meant that Tom had reached the outskirts of the small west-coast town of Westport.
His father always said Clew Bay was the most beautiful sight in the world on a fine spring morning.
Tom's attention was taken not by the panoramic view of the bay slowly disappearing from view behind the architecture of the town, but by the figure of a young girl about a hundred yards down the hill. The girl attracting his attention appeared to be carrying a wicker basket which was swinging in her right hand as if she hadn't a care in the world.

Tom's curiosity was telling him to urge the donkey to go faster to catch up to the young lady. Wisely, after what happened on the boreen, he decided that travelling faster than a brisk walking pace down a hill on an uneven surface was too risky with the six crates of fresh eggs on the cart. Besides there were other the commuters to contend with, all picking out the best track on the journey to and from the port.

Tom was getting closer and could see that the young girl with the basket had shoulder length auburn hair which was glinting in sunlight as it lifted in the light Atlantic breeze.

Tom was by nature a shy lad, but this was no time to miss an opportunity, the auburn hair stopped and bent over to fasten a shoelace. Just as Tom caught her up she picked up her basket, flicked her hair, and continued on her way unaware she was being observed. Tom adjusted the speed of the cart to match the pace of the auburn hair and offered the young lady a ride into town. Auburn hair continued walking.

Tom went ahead and stopped the cart, this time a few yards in ahead, giving the girl time to consider the situation. Again, auburn hair continued walking. Realising the offer of a ride was a lost cause Tom decided to engage in conversation.

---

[4]   *Drumlin, a low oval mound, typically one of a group, as in the small islands in Clew Bay.*

'Hello, my names Tom, what do they call you'? He enquired, struggling to hold the donkey to a slow walking pace on their way down the hill.

No reply.

Tom repeated the question a little louder.

Again no reply.

Just as he was about to give up.

'Honor, but I prefer Nora,' she said softly, her pale green eyes avoiding his gaze.

Her cheeks took on a pleasing glow, adding to the attraction as Tom strove to keep the conversation going while controlling the cart.

'I haven't seen you before when I do this run?'

After a long pause, she replied weakly.

'I came here from England last Sunday, to live with my auntie.'

'And who might your auntie be?' Tom asked with a cheeky smile, sounding more confident.

'Bridie Murphy, that's her farm you've just passed at the top of the hill.'

'So you'd be Nora Murphy. Where ya goin with that basket Nora Murphy?'

'You ask a lot of questions,' Nora replied with a coy smile.

'That's because I like what I see,' Tom's face flushed bright red as he couldn't believe what he had just said.

His embarrassment was short-lived when Nora pointed with the basket to the open door of a shop and said.

'This is where I'm going with my basket.'

Tom stopped the cart realising they had arrived at the bakery.

Four days later on his next run to Westport Quay Tom timed his journey to ensure that he passed Murphy farm at about the same time with the hope of seeing Nora. Sure enough, there she was a few yards ahead walking down the hill with the wicker basket swinging in her right hand.

This time Tom was able to learn more about the attractive young girl that captured his attention as she walked to the bakery.

It turned out that Nora's parents had moved to England and were lodging with another Mayo family in an already crowded terrace close to the Liverpool docks. Her ageing aunt Bride Murphy had recently been widowed, and Nora, encouraged by her mother had offered to live at the farm for a few weeks while she recovered from her bereavement. When her aunt was able to cope with the farm on her own, Nora was to return to her parents in Liverpool.

On his next journey to Westport, Tom was a little earlier than usual. He thought he'd missed Nora with no sight of her on the road. His heart sank, until he spotted her walking towards him down the boreen from the farm.

She pretended not to see him keeping her eyes set straight ahead.

As she came closer Tom noticed the hint of a smile giving him the confidence to offer her a ride.

'It wouldn't be right, you know that Tom' she said reminding him of the custom.

'Yee'll be OK sitting sideways on the end'

To Tom's relief she accepted and clambered up beside him placing her basket on the narrow seat, making a respectable space between them.

This time Nora started the conversation,

'I had a letter from me ma today', she whispered shyly.

Tom a little surprised by Nora's speaking first just nodded and before he could reply, Nora continued.

'Me da's been taken on at the docks in Liverpool, the foreman's from over here; he recommended da for the job.'

'Have they found anywhere to live?' Tom enquired trying to sound interested.

'There's an empty house in the street where they're lodging, they're moving in next week'.

'Does that mean you'll be joining them?' Tom asked hoping Nora would say no.

Before she could answer the aroma of freshly baked bread filled the air.

Tom...so engrossed with Nora's future plans...hadn't realised they were near the bakery.

Still waiting for an answer, Tom stopped the cart by the bakery door.

To Tom's delight for the first time Nora looked directly into his eyes and said with a mischievous smile.

'Ma thinks I should stay a few more weeks to help auntie recover from her loss, it'll give them time to settle into their new house as well.'

After a pause that seemed to last forever Nora turned, smiled, and waved tentatively while Tom watched the wicker basket and auburn tresses disappear.

Chapter 6

A Better Life

At the Lockan crossroads the donkey's nose pointed towards the market town of Ballingar. It was usual for Tom to take a shorter more direct route when delivering the latest batch of eggs to the exporter at Westport Quay. Today, Tom had promised his best friend Martin Cassidy a ride to Westport to catch the Steam Packet to England.

Tom's regular journey delivering eggs to the port is usually made alone with only his thoughts and the donkey for company, today will be the last chance he has to see Martin and wish him farewell before he leaves home to seek work in England.

The Lockan crossroads two miles from the town of Balingar is the location of the only blacksmiths forge in the area, and is owned by Dan Collins a master smith servicing the needs of the populous for miles around.

Passing by the smithy to Tom's surprise he noticed no sign of activity, the doors were closed and barred and not a wisp of smoke from the chimney.

That's unusual thought Tom, Dan's normally up and about by now with the forge belching black smoke from a newly lit fire.

A mile farther along the Ballingar road the newly built 'Church of our Lady' came into view and Tom's thoughts turned to his friend Martin. Martin is taking the Steam Packet to England, the long way around the coast of Ireland to the port of Liverpool in the hope of finding work in one of the many factories and dockyards that line the banks of the river Mersey.

Many of his friends have already left with their families; cajoled by the landlord of their shack to flee the desperate situation they found themselves in after he cruelly raised the rent leaving them no other choice but to emigrate.

On the streets and in the bars and markets around Ballingar, Martin often heard from friends and relations that have made the journey to North

America constantly saying, 'I'm off away to America, nothing for me here, my cousin in Chicago lives like a lord.' A few weeks later they would take the road to the ports of Westport, Sligo, or Dublin to seek what they hoped would be a better life. Almost every day Martin would hear neighbours telling of relations or acquaintances making a new life across the water, pointing west to America or east to England as if they could see their friends in their new abode. One mother, grieving to the point of starvation after her favourite son had left for America, summoned all of her remaining strength to trek up the holy mountain...Crough Patrick, looking west beyond Clew Bay imagining she could see her son across the wide Atlantic Ocean while preying to the holy saint to keep him safe.

Martin saw mothers, their eyes sparkling with tears of pride; showing neighbours cherished finger worn letters describing life in Boston, New York or cities in England where many emigrants from Ireland's west coast have settled.

'Sure there's a good living to be had working the dockyards of New York', or 'go to Manchester son, you will be taken on in those mills, cotton mills, there's lots of them cryin out for workers.'

The opportunity to send dollars home from labouring in Boston or pound notes from stoking boilers in the Black Country, must be better than breaking your back scratching a living on the stony soil of Mayo, Martin thought.

When a relative or friend had funds enough to return home for a wedding, funeral or some other special occasion for the next few days the streets and bars of Ballingar would be buzzing with stories of life in New York, Liverpool, or London.

'You'll be well fed in America or England,' would be heard as poverty often turned to hunger in many parts of rural Ireland.

For the last few years, in the autumn, Martin's father Tim had journeyed with Tom's father Joe and other farmers to Staffordshire England to work as a 'Harvest Men'...the extra labour to help bring in the harvest on farms.

One winter's night sitting around the comfort of the turf fire Tim Cassidy told of the time when he and the other harvest men early on a Sunday morning attended mass at Catholic chapel a few miles away in Bilston, the nearest town. A town with tall chimneys filling the air with black smoke, giving the streets and buildings a dark appearance, so much that they call the area the 'Black Country'. Foundrys, coal mines, iron mills and small sheds in back streets making all sorts of metal objects.

Stories like these helped Martin make up his mind and after thinking it over carefully he decided where he wanted to emigrate to, telling his best friend Tom, 'for sure I'm going to England but not to the 'Black Country'

I'm going to Liverpool, it's a port from there I can go anywhere in the world.'

Martin tried to imagine what it would be like living in a big city like Liverpool.

What it would be like working in a factory or labouring in a dockyard.

What it would be like living in a place without fields, mountains and bogs where turf for your fire is free.

What would it be like away from my family and all my friends in this town.

Would it be a better life? I'll take my chances, anyway I can always come back to Ballingar.

Chapter 7

Martin Cassidy

Thomas Walsh and Martin Cassidy were born in the same year a month apart, in houses a fifty long paces from each other. They spent most of their early years playing and learning together and were sometimes mistaken for brothers despite Martin's light brown hair and smaller five foot six stature compared to Tom's taller five ten and dark hair.

At the age of five they began their schooling on the same day at Ballingar National School, walking down the boreen with the older children to the one room school on the outskirts of the town. They would often be chastised for dawdling on their way home from school, knowing chores await them at the farm. One of their regular distractions was when they stopped at the smithy to watch Dan Collins the blacksmith at work shoeing a horse or repairing a plough.

When not working on the family farm they spent the little spare time they had playing in the fields and in the sparsely wooded copse nearby, the trees providing the materials to make swords, guns and bows and arrows. Their favourite game was playing French soldiers coming to free of Ireland of English rule, chasing the English back across the Irish sea, only in their game unlike what they were taught in school the French always win.

In their teenage years Martin and Tom, began to take an interest in the young colleen's of the parish. Only to find that in the hard times of evictions and near famine, just as a relationship with a girl began to develop the girl and her family emigrated to England or America.

The Cassidy family was forced to leave the townland of Knockaun when the absentee English landlord racked up the already high rent to a point where they had to choose between eating or paying the rent.

After appealing...to no avail...to the landlord's agent for more time to find the money he owed, Martin's father Tim Cassidy out of desperation made the journey into town to plead with the local priest for help, showing him the eviction notice stating the Cassidy family would be evicted in seven days time because of non payment of rent.

Tim explained to the priest that there had been a massive hike in the rent and it was the cause of the dire circumstances the family found themselves in.

With a benevolent nod of his head; the priest told Tim that he was well aware of the situation in his and other parishes in rural Ireland. After a pause to consider how he could help Tim and his family the priest placed his hand on Tim's shoulder and promised to see what he could do by making some enquires in the town.

'Try not to worry too much Timothy, I know of something that might suit your family, I realise it's urgent, I'll see to it tonight.' Two days later the priest returned to the beleaguered family with a letter offering the position as caretaker at the Ballingar Courthouse, a position that included the adjacent small cottage.

Within twenty-four hours of the Cassidy's vacating their house the landlord's agent had it taken down rendering it uninhabitable, leaving just a stone shell.

In an effort to win over the neighbouring cottiers, the agent offered stone from the ruins of the Cassidy house to the remaining tenants to repair their houses and boundary walls, which was immediately refused in the knowledge that if they used just one stone they would be ostracised by the community and become a target of the growing resistance movement The Land League.

As a reminder of the injustice of the feudal absentee landlord, the residents followed the tradition of other evictions by leaving the shell of the house standing for all to see.

Chapter 8

The Cassidy House

When Tom arrived at the Cassidy house the aroma of food being cooked, drifted through the open door of a nearby property, making him wish he'd been able to eat a more substantial breakfast, other than the remains of a loaf and a cup of water.

The brown door of the Cassidy house with it's peeling paint revealing a previous colour beneath gave it a sad appearance, as if it too was sorry to see Martin leave.

A bleary eyed Martin emerged from the dimly lit interior of the house and waved to Tom with a gesture that said give me a minute. The previous night, Martin, Tom and a few friends bid Martin farewell with what is known in Ireland as an 'American Wake'[5] at Campbell's Bar, and Tom's head was still feeling the effects of the late night celebrations. Now would be a good time to check the ropes again, Tom thought jumping down to inspect the egg boxes at the back of the cart when Martin's parents appeared, his father first then his mother dabbing a tear from her eye with her shawl.

Breaking away from his mother's arms, Martin took his place alongside his friend at the front of the cart.

Just as they were about to leave Martin's mother let out a loud heart rendering cry followed by. 'Stay safe son, send a letter so I'll know yer alright son.'

---

[5]   *An American Wake is held to celebrate a friend or family member immigrating usually to America.*

His ageing mother found it hard to accept that her youngest, son was leaving home to live in a far off place, even though almost every family in the town has a son or daughter living away from home.

Martin jumped down from the cart hugged his mother and said, 'Don't be frettin ma, I WILL write, and send some money when I find a job.'

Martin's father stepped forward put his hand on his son's shoulder and in a low voice said…as he had said to his other children before they left home.

'Good luck son look after yourself don't forget to write it will be a great comfort to your mother.'

'Yes da, I won't forget, don't worry, I'll write as soon as I'm settled.'

With a tear in his eye Martin waved to his parents until the cart turned the corner into Main Street, continuing to look back long after they were out of sight.

The small market town of Ballingar was beginning to come alive. The smell of freshly cooked food and newly ignited turf confused Tom's senses again, making him feel hungry and queasy at the same time. Familiar faces appeared in the low doorways of the grass-thatched cottages lining the street.

A familiar pungent earthy odour wafted under their noses as a black-shawled old lady crossed the road with an iron shovel at arm's length carrying a wad of glowing turf to re-ignite the dying embers in a neighbour's hearth.

A brief halt to allow a gaggle of geese driven by a barefoot girl from out of town to pass by on her way to the market.

Hardware shopkeeper Henry Meagher once ramrod straight, now in his late seventies...his back bowed like the few trees that survive the wind-swept slopes of Croagh Patrick...was arranging his wares along the narrow walkway in front of his hardware shop, paused to give them a wave.

A few minutes later with the town behind them the boys were heading back to the Lockan crossroads. Apart from greeting a solitary farmer walking his horses from the fields for another day working the land Martin was unusually quiet. Tom, realising that this would be a difficult journey for his friend...sitting next to him staring blankly at nothing in particular...decided it was wiser to leave him to his thoughts.

After five minutes of silence Martin was the first to speak.

'They're on their own now, if things work out I'll make enough money to pay for them to visit me in England, that's if I can persuade them to leave Ballingar.'

More silence, then.

'Oh yes Tom I almost forgot, I went to see Father Quinn on Sunday to tell him I was leaving for England, he gave me a letter to give to Father Byrne in Castlebar it's on our way, hope you don't mind calling there, he said Father Byrne has contacts in England that can help me find a job.'

'Campbell's bar was good craic last night, you made the most of your last night in town!' Tom said changing the subject.

'The boys gave you a send off to remember, my ribs are sore with laughing and my head hurts like hell,' Tom added trying to hold his ribs and the reins at the same time.'

Martin reacted with a barely perceptible nod of the head, still thinking about what he was leaving behind...his ageing parents, friends and a town where he knew almost everyone...for what. An uncertain future?

Travelling in silence at a leisurely pace along the quiet stretch of the road and nursing a hangover lulled Tom into a false sense of security until one of the cart's wheels found an extra deep hole in the road. Using the reins to steady himself he pulled back so hard it caused the straining donkey to emit a loud rasping noise followed by a foul odour. That did it. That broke the spell.

'The feckin donkey farted,' Martin laughed covering his face with his hand.

Chapter 9

Daniel Collins, Blacksmith

At the Lockan crossroads Tom stopped the cart for Martin to call at the Smithy...a place that holds happy memories for them both...to allow Martin to say farewell to Dan the blacksmith.

Daniel Collins an upright man with muscular arms bearing the scars of many years working with hot iron. He is the man whose favour everyone liked to cultivate. At some time or other almost everyone in the parish and its environs will need his services, whether to repair a plough, shoe a horse, or to make an iron gate, the blacksmith is the man they turn to. This dependence gives Dan an advantage over his peers, making him one of the most respected men in the community.

Dan's wife Anne is a tall slim woman with jet black hair...now showing signs of grey...who spends most of her time raising four hungry children as well as helping Dan with his business. Since they were wed early every Wednesday morning Anne prepares her husband's clothes for his weekly visit to the livestock market at Ballingar. At ten-o-clock sharp Dan locks the smithy's doors, saddles his grey gelding, changes into his best suit and rides the two-miles into town.

The Ballingar livestock market is more than a business day; it is also a social occasion. Farmers living in outlying townlands and villages look to market day as an opportunity, not only to buy and sell livestock, but also to catch up with family news and events and Dan being at the hub of the community has a lot of news to exchange.

Dan's smithy is ideally located at the north side of the Lockan crossroads alongside the Ballingar road attracting trade from farmers as far as twenty miles away, such is Dan's reputation as a 'Master Smith.'
Elm trees and a thick holly hedge protect one side of the holding from the wind that blows off Mayo's Atlantic coast.

The Collins family dwell in a single story stone house with a newly thatched roof at the back of the smithy. It sits in a quarter of an acre of carefully tilled garden with a large turf store near to the house...some farmers can only afford to pay by barter offering turf for the house fire or farm produce in return for urgent repairs to a plough or cart. A fresh water stream fed from a nearby spring runs along the boundary serving the needs of both the household and the Forge.

Dan being the eldest son, inherited the three-room house and Smithy when his father passed on and is hoping the line will continue with his eldest son. The forge where Dan plies his trade is a typical Irish smithy; learning his trade at his father's side being able to shoe a horse from the age of ten, starting with a donkey before graduating to shoeing horses of all sizes.

At one end of the workshop is the forge alongside a large hand bellows, it's long wooden handle polished over many years by hands pumping the air necessary to force the fire to maximum heat. Two paces away near the centre of the room is a large anvil fastened to a round wooden block cut from the trunk of an ancient oak still showing the remains of it's bark. On the opposite wall next to an iron quenching tank is an old hand powered sandstone wheel...used for fettling and sharpening...mounted on a cast-iron stand with a handle wide enough for two hands.

Covering the remaining spaces on the dusty lime washed walls are iron racks supporting various hand tools, most handed down from previous generations of blacksmiths. Rows of tongs with mouths formed to grip metal of any shape or size. Chisels and dies with thick wire handles used to cut and forge the hot iron into useful implements, their tops mushroomed where the hammer has hit them countless times.

On fine summer days, the double wooden doors of the smithy are opened wide, giving passers-by a perfect view of the forge within. Sometimes they might stop to catch up on the latest news, whilst watching the skill of a master craftsman turn a piece of iron into a useful object. Others wait for a quick repair, or to collect a finished article. Many just pause on their way to town to wonder at the sight of a muscular broad-shouldered craftsman wearing a sleeveless vest, protected only by a leather apron, performing what seemed like magical pyrotechnics illuminating the interior of the workshop with the sparkling iron when it's withdrawn from the forge.

Tom Walsh, Martin Cassidy, and other boys from Knockaun liked to vary their route on their way home from Ballingar National School. Some days they would pass the Forge, other days they would pick their way across the bog or dare each other to walk through the churchyard on the dark winter evenings.

For youths like Tom and Martin, the Smithy was a place of wonder and a place to linger and pass the time before going home to their daily chores on the farm.

Blacksmith Dan Collins would say to the boys, 'If you're staying here you can make yourselves useful by sweeping the floor or tidy the racks of tools.' Which the boys did as fast as possible giving them time to play when Mr Collins was working in the yard repairing a plough or other large implement.

The boys invented a competition to see who could balance the sledgehammer on their foot...with the shaft on the foot and the head in the air...for the longest.

They found this great fun until one boy from Ballingar tried to balance the hammer on his chin and it slipped giving him a thick lip and breaking two front teeth.

'That'll stop you whistling at the girls.' Dan joked as his wife tended to the boy,

Martin liked the place so much he often told Tom he wanted to be a blacksmith like Mr Collins. They both liked the place, the smell of the horses, the forge and the hot iron, all combined to make a comforting warm atmosphere. Watching Mr Collins shoe a horse, or forge a new part for a plough, fascinated the boys. How did he know which of the hundreds of tools to use, and why did a horse stay calm while he hammered nails into it's hooves?

Although they saw Dan make a new tyre for a cartwheel many times, that is what impressed Tom and Martin the most.

They watched him work out the size of the tyre by measuring the circumference of the wooden wheel, before rolling a length of flat wrought iron into a circle, to a diameter slightly smaller than the wooden wheel. Dan's striker,[6] Mick Fox, pumped away at the bellows carefully preparing the fire to heat the ends of the iron tyre by making a small mound of blazing bright red hot ashes. Mick, sweating the previous night's ale, continued pumping away at the bellows until the fire was white-hot.

After placing the metal ring into the fierce white heat of the fire Dan waited until the abutting ends were almost melting. Using his years of experience he withdrew the metal from the fire to carefully hammer the abutting ends of the tyre together over the beak of the anvil, until they welded together to make a complete wrought iron tyre. To finish the job, the joint was then fettled smooth on the grindstone.

After double-checking the diameter to ensure the steel band was a good shrink-fit to grip the wheel tightly when quenched, the ring is reheated on an open fire set in the yard close to the wooden wheel laid down on bricks. To fit the iron tyre to the wooden wheel once it had expanded, Dan and Mick lifted it from the fire using purpose made tongs and lowered it quickly over the wheel. A bucket of cold quenching water is thrown on the iron band causing it to contract quickly creating clouds of steam hissing and

---

6

wood creaking as the new iron tyre griped the wooden wheel tightening onto the spokes making it ready for many more years of service.

[6] A blacksmith's striker is the blacksmith's third hand, he is the man who strikes the various tools with the sledgehammer as well as pumping the bellows and other duties in the smithy.

Chapter 10

Mick Fox Storyteller

During the dark winter nights gathered around the cosy warmth of the hearth in front of a glowing turf fire, families would listen to stories related by elderly relatives or sometimes visit a neighbour's house for a night of stories, singing and dancing. An itinerant storyteller on his way from town to town might stay in a house for a couple of nights, paying for his board by telling stories from his diverse repertoire.

Tom and Martin never tired of listening to a good story even though they'd heard most of them many times. A farmer might stop at the smithy to pass on news heard while visiting a market miles away, or just to hear the blacksmith relate a story passed down through the generations.

Ghost stories and tales about unexplained happenings were the most popular.

Mick Fox the blacksmiths striker has a reputation as one of Mayo's best storytellers; honing his art on the visitors to the forge, often telling his yarns in instalments if they were particularly busy.

On the most popular drinking nights in Ballingar town, Mick was always in demand for a good story. He would often be seen going from bar to bar, some nights visiting almost every bar in town; it was his way of obtaining free ale.

Tom and Martin heard Mick relate his wondrous tales when he called at Campbell's their favourite bar.

Mick rarely bought a drink, usually finishing the night singing to himself as he rolled his way home.

So popular were his stories they were asked for time and again.

Eager listeners would say.

'Let's have the one about the old lady with the magic stick or the one about the little man in the tree.'

Tom and Martin were there when he related the one about the 'Silent Army'.

Feigning reluctance, standing to his full five foot six height Mick would take a deep breath…enough to expand his barrel chest…slowly look around the room, take an extra large swallow of ale, clear his throat and begin.

The Silent Army

'The event I am about to relate happened many years ago. It frightened me so much I can remember it as if it were yesterday.'

To ensure he had the attention of the crowd, Mick paused slowly scanning the listeners with a wide-eyed in fixed stare.

'It was late in September, just before midnight.
The full moon lit up the hillside as if it was midday causing the few trees to cast long shadows like fingers pointing the way as I made my way home.
Occasional passing clouds dimmed the moonlight like snuffing candles, then one by one they come to life lighting the path as the clouds continue on their way.'

'I'd been checking my Poteen[7] on the high bog, as well as filling a few bottles to take to market...it's not there now so don't go looking for it...and was walking up the hill thinking how bright the moon was.
The silence was broken only by a light wind blowing through the trees and the call of an owl in the distance.
As I passed the three-acre field...the one with the standing stones...out of the corner of my eye I saw something move.
At first I thought it was the shadow of the clouds passing in front of the moon.'

Then a pause as he picks up his jar, looks deeply into it to increase the tension and takes another swig of ale.

'Gradually, I could just make out the shapes of men on horseback coming towards me.
Thinking it might be the Guards and not wanting to be caught with the bottles stashed in my coat, ya know the one with extra pockets, special for bottles.
I looked around for somewhere to hide, there was nowhere.
As they got closer I sensed something wasn't right; not a sound could be heard, no talking, no sound from the horses, nothing but silence.
I froze to the spot, shaking with fear, me few old teeth rattling louder than the bottles in me pocket.

---

[7]   *Poteen, alcohol made illicitly typically from potatoes.*

I dropped to the ground, almost cried out as the bottles pressed into me ribs, leaving me bruised for days.'

'Slowly the riders emerged from a kind of damp foggy mist; I could see that they were soldiers, very weary looking soldiers with their bodies bowed over the horses.
Not like those English down the road in the barracks, these had ragged red uniforms with gold braid and red hats with a black brush on the front.
The horse's heads were drooped low. Where the eyes should be there was nothing, just empty sockets and although it was a very cold night there was no breath from their nostrils, they looked as tired as their riders.'

Mick then paused for another swig of ale then wiped his lips with the back of his hand.

'French soldiers,' Tom whispered.

'Shush I know, I remember this story,' Martin replied grumpily.

'A cold chill went through me body.' Mick continued.
'I thought I must be dreaming till I felt the pain from the bottles pressing against me chest.
All was not as it should be,' Mick said with another wide-eyed stare around the room.

'Frozen to the spot with fear they came marching on towards me.
Tramping wearily behind the horsemen about two dozen foot soldiers, the two in the front rank tapping a single beat on kettle drums, not a sound...silent feckin drums?
All their heads were bowed...like the horses...most with their uniforms in tatters.
Not a sound was to be heard, even though the hooves of the horses were uncovered.
Looked as if they were floating a couple of inches above the ground.
They were coming straight at me. I thought they would trample me into the ground.
*I said a silent prayer, a 'Hail Mary'...*He says a prayer and crosses himself as if it was happening.
'With hooves coming closer and closer I wanted the ground to open up,'

Then with fixed stare of mock fear in his eyes, Mick looked around the room at the enthralled listeners; slowly picked up his jar, lifted it to his lips and almost drained it.

'Now where was I?'

'Me heart beating like a bohran gone mad, and the hooves less than ten feet from me I could see that under the red hats they had no face just a sallow grey skull with strips of skin hanging like a torn curtain.

Faceless feckin soldiers they've come to take me to the next world...shall I stay or run?'

His face contorted in mock fear as he continued the tale with even more agitated fervour his voice rising to a dramatic crescendo, then suddenly and slowly in a soft voice.

'The leading riders entered the stone circle which seemed to light up, the light got brighter until the centre was glowing with the light of a thousand church candles.

I watched shaking with fear for what seemed like an age as they entered the centre of the circle.

Gradually one by one they vanished as if swallowed up by the light, horsemen and the foot soldiers gone.

Suddenly it was dark again, as if a great wind had blown out all the candles at once.

Everything was back to normal it was like they had been swallowed up by a feckin big hole in the centre of the stone circle.

'Where the had they gone?'

I was shaking so much I grabbed one of the bottles lining me coat.

Now was a good time to try the Poteen.

Half a bottle later I recovered enough to look closely inside the stone circle to see where they'd gone.

Nothing had changed there was no sign of how they could have disappeared.

Two more swigs from the bottle and I was ready to carry on...still shakin...for home.'

The next day I went to the field with the stones. Everything looked the same...no hoof marks in the grass...till I went into the stone circle.'

With a twisted smile Mick paused again for effect then looked around the room sticking his head forward to emphasise the look of wonder on his face.

'In the centre of the stone circle the ground was bare, grass was had gone and around the stones the grass was black, scorched like someone had set a fire.'

Suddenly lifting his glass he burst into song.

'The French they came and chased them out and Castlebar is free. Castlebar is free boys. Castlebar is free'.

At this point Mick struggled to his feet, downed the remaining ale in his jar and retired to the back yard, leaving the listeners to wonder at the meaning of the tale.

33

Chapter 11

The League

'That's unusual, look Tom the smithy doors are closed, I wanted to say goodbye to Dan, he said to call on my way to Westport,' Martin said when they arrived at the Lockan crossroads.

Just as they were about to continue their journey Tom Dan's wife Anne appeared with two of her youngest children.

'Good morning Mrs Collins, is Dan around' Tom inquired.

'Called away in a hurry, something about repairing a plough, he sent Mick Fox off with a message, the strange thing is he's not taken any tools.'

'Perhaps the farmer had his own tools; we stopped, to say goodbye Mrs Collins, I'm leaving for England today.' Martin said, trying to justify Dan's reason for leaving without the means to do his work.

'He should be home soon to open up, I'll tell him when he gets back. Good luck in England Martin,' Anne said gathering her children to her apron to wave goodbye to Martin as Tom urged the donkey in the direction of Castlebar and Westport.

Gradually, little by little Tom's memory of Martin's last night in Ballingar before leaving slowly took shape, however, something seemed to be bothering him. Something was not quite right. His beer befuddled head tried to remember the scene in the back room of Campbell's bar.

He remembered brothers Will, and John Rooney...nicknamed 'The Firedogs' by the regulars because they claim seats either side of the turf fire...sitting there lighting their clay pipes with paper spills crafted from old newspapers. (Although they are not twins the Rooney brothers looked almost identical. Most people identified them by the groove in what is left of their front teeth, caused by gripping a clay pipe. John has the groove on the left and Will on the right.)

Trying hard to remember the events of the previous night, Tom slowly scanned the rest of the room in his mind's eye, dredging the picture of the night's celebrations from the hazy depths of his memory.

He remembered that most of the folk in the room were the familiar faces of regulars apart from the two strangers standing at the end of the counter. They entered the bar late in the evening, ignoring the rest of the drinkers looking around the room as if expecting trouble the settled at the end of the bar with their heads almost touching as if not wanting to be heard. After ordering their drinks they engaged conversation with proprietor Paddy Campbell, one leaning over the counter whispering in Paddy's ear. Tom strained to remember their faces, two more opposite characters you could not imagine, one tall and slim, with grey hair, and thick grey moustache to match, the other, average height with broad shoulders, a broken nose, and very little hair apart from a short scruffy grey beard which gave the appearance of an upside-down head. Tom's last recollection was of the two strangers following Paddy Campbell to his living room through a door marked private. He remembered them entering the room with their heads slightly bowed as if the bearer of bad news. Just before the door closed Tom had a brief glimpse of an outstretched arm, greeting the two strangers. He remembered thinking he'd seen that arm somewhere before.

Whose arm was it? There was something familiar about it.

Why did Paddy Campbell take two strangers to his private room?

Tom's head was still suffering the after effects of the previous night, much too scrambled for puzzles.

'What were you saying about stopping to see the priest in Castlebar.'

Tom said, awakening Martin from his own private thoughts.

'Ah yes, well err, err.' Martin struggled to find the words after ten minutes of thinking about his uncertain future.

'You heard about the landlords constantly putting up the rents, rent-racking they call it.
Well…you know…just as we was thrown out of our place last year, my uncle Tim and his family were cleared off their farm on the other side of Ballingar last week after the rent was increased to almost double twice in a year, leaving him no way of paying.

Eventually, rather than go to the Gombeen and borrow money...money he knew he had no chance of repaying...he had to choose between feeding his family and paying the rent by selling anything of value, the cattle, the donkey and cart, and as a last resort, some of the better pieces of furniture.

He said he would do anything to feed his family. Things were that desperate.

His close neighbours old Jim Duffy and his wife took them in, all six of them, they're still there all of them in three small rooms.

Jim Duffy's wife good...as she was...expected the worse and made them as comfortable she could.'

Martin paused to allow Tom to think about what he had related, then continued.

'Jim Duffy and his son Ned are now members of a new organisation called The Land League and after what his family had been through it didn't take much persuading for Uncle Tim to join.'

'I heard about the evictions and heard my da talking about a Land League starting up to stop evictions. Is that what do they do? 'Who's in it'? Tom enquired.

'It was formed to help farmers like Uncle Tim and to stop the English landlords that don't live or belong in this country clearing people off land they've been farming for generations.

At the last league meeting they talked about organising events to raise money to help those struggling to pay their rent. Another proposal suggested is for all local business people to refuse to sell goods or give a service...like shoeing a horse or selling goods...to anyone who works for the landlord at the big house' or on his land. It's already started to happen in some parts. On some of the big estates they are having to have some food brought in from England, and take their horse out of the area travelling miles to have them shod because local smiths are refusing to work for them.'

'When I was in Westport last week I heard about agents asking people to work for them and offering good money, was told they had their bullyboys from England with them for protection.

'Is it working, the ban on working for the big estates?' Tom asked trying to concentrate.

'Well, it's early days yet, the English have brought in extra troops from England to try to stop the protests. They know that as the evictions continue our men are becoming more organised and joining the League. New Land League committees are being formed in all parts of the country. There's talk of cartloads of Orange-men coming down from Antrim and other parts of the north to work on the estates and help the militia when clearing our people of the land they've farmed for generations.

We're all affected in some way by the evictions. If the English want to harvest their crops, it's going to cost them dearly. Lord Langton in the 'big house' has set up his own smithy and bakery shipping in a blacksmith and baker from his estate in England. They're saying anyone that refuses to give a service will be charged with criminal conspiracy, whatever that is.'

'Yes but what's all that got to do with the church apart from looking after the homeless people?' Tom interrupted.

'Well on Sunday after mass I went to see Father Quinn for his blessing, and to tell him I was going to England.

He said he was sorry to see me leave and would I call to see Father Byrne in Castlebar on the way to Westport to give him a letter.'

'But what's the priest got to do with 'The League'?'

Father Quinn runs the Ballingar branch of the 'Land League', he's the chairman and Father Byrne is the chairman of the Castlebar 'Land League' branch, the biggest in Mayo.

Father Quinn is looking for new members to strengthen the Ballingar branch; we have to stop the evictions; would you like to join Tom? You could take my place.'

Tom thought a while, trying to make sense of what Martin had related before answering angrily.

'I was stopped last week at a roadblock set up by English soldiers. They searched the cart, opened all feckin the boxes...the bastards, broke no eggs though, said they were looking for guns. That was the third time this month I've been stopped always between Castlebar and Westport.

One fecker looked at me with a bit of a smile on his ugly face as if he knew me, never seen him before, very strange I could have sworn he winked.'

'Perhaps he liked the look of ya,' Martin teased.

'More like something in his eye,' Tom replied still thinking about the harassment he endured when going about his legitimate business of collecting and delivering eggs to the port.

'Yes I'll join the League and our Michael might be persuaded to join as well.'

'Too late Tom, he's already joined,' Martin said with a wry smile.

'That's where he's been going at night, the sly fecker; I thought he was chasing after woman'. Tom laughed.

'He and a few others from the League are being called 'Moonlighters'; all operating in the Ballingar area,' Martin added.

'What's a Moonlighter? I've overheard Mick talk about them to his friend but he always changes the subject when I ask.'

'He's kept it from you Tom because he's sworn to secrecy, the less you know the better. Now that you're joining you'll find out anyway.

  Moonlighters go out at night making life difficult for anyone co-operating with the landlords that evict our people, you know the ones in the 'big house' like the one in Westport. They go out at night and threaten his workers with serious injury for working his land, torch his barns and maim his cattle, anything to get even for the misery they cause. We're fighting for fair rents[8] , a fair rent for a house and a few acres of land where we've lived for generations. I'm not saying our Ballingar branch members go quite that far. Father Quinn is against violence except in self defence, anything that will help stop the evictions,' Martin added passionately.

'When I join, I'd like to go out with them at night but I don't think my da would want me to, I don't think he'd risk two sons being caught breaking the law, he's always thinking about the business.' Tom said trying to concentrate on steering the cart around the potholes.

After the passionate talk of the Land League the conversation between the boys dried up; Martin's was thinking about their next stop at Castlebar to see Father Byrne and how the infamous priest would receive them.

Tom had other things on his mind.

---

[8]   *The land league fought for the three f's, Fair rent, fixed tenure, and free sale.*

Chapter 12

Nora Murphy

Around the next bend the smoke-laden haze hanging over the town of Castlebar came into view bringing with it the comforting earthy smell of the turf fires warming the hearths of the town.

Tom's mood lightened at the thought of seeing Nora, It shouldn't take long to deliver the letter to Father Byrne, and then we'll be on our way to Westport and would soon be passing the Murphy farm, he thought smiling to himself.

For days while travelling the to local farms collecting eggs and working in the barn packing eggs, the auburn-haired Nora occupied Tom's thoughts more and more to the point where he questioned how much he liked her. If I cannot stop thinking about her, if I think about her all the time it must be love, or is it all I know is I can't wait to see her again? He thought trying to concentrate on grading and packing the eggs safely in the straw lined boxes.

Other girls with whom Tom started a close friendship had left with their family to seek work abroad; making Tom reluctant to admit to himself that he was fond of Nora. Perhaps more than fond, perhaps in love. People around him were beginning to notice a change in his behaviour. His mother concerned about his moods and unusual demeanour asked.

'What's wrong with you Thomas walking around in a dream staring at nothing in particular, are you feeling unwell or is it a girl you're frettin over?'

'I'm grand ma, honest, just leave me be.' Tom would snap back.

On his next run to Westport, hoping to see Nora again, Tom stopped the cart near to the boreen leading to the Murphy farm and pretended to adjust the donkey's bridle until one passer-by thinking he was in trouble stopped asking to help.

Fending off the offer of assistance Tom continued on his way thinking that his beloved Nora had left the farm, and must be some way ahead of him on her daily walk to town. In his eagerness to catch up with her, he urged the ever-willing donkey to go faster than was comfortable along the uneven road, putting the fragile cargo in danger. To Tom's delight, in the distance he could just make out the figure of a young girl with red hair, a red plaid shawl over her shoulders and a wicker basket, walking slowly down the steepest section of the hill. 'Is it Nora'? He whispered to himself.

It was Nora. She must have heard the cart trundling ever closer down the hill, and was turning to look back, at the same time slowing her pace to allow Tom to catch up.

'I looked out for you, you'll have to give a sign to let me know you're on your way to town, it'll save me waiting and give us more time to talk.' Tom said softly.

'What do you mean a sign?'

Nora laughed as Tom stroked his chin like a wise old man stroking his beard.

'We need to think of something to let me know you're on your way to town,'

Tom said still stroking his chin, encouraged by Nora's reaction.

'I'll put a stick on the big marker stone at the end of our road.' Nora said looking at Tom with an encouraging smile.

'Good idea but not a stick it might blow away it would have to be something heavier more like a stone.'

It was settled, every time Nora went to town she would place a small stone on the white marker stone at the entrance to the boreen indicating she was on her way to town.

To Tom's delight on his next journey delivering eggs to Westport he noticed that Nora sat a little closer, giving him the confidence to offer to take her nearer to her aunt's farm by taking the cart up the boreen.

At a point where the boreen was shielded by an overhanging tree Tom asked Nora would she like to take the reins.

When Nora moved closer to take control of the cart, Tom put his arms around her to allow his hands to hold Nora's and the reins.

'Like this,' he encouraged giving her soft hands a loving squeeze.

Nora edged closer closing what little gap remained then turned to look directly into his eyes giving Tom the courage to hold her tighter and whisper softly.

'Do you have to go back to England?'

Nora's reply was a tender kiss on his cheek whilst tightly holding his hand.

Instinctively, with his heart pounding he held her tighter, kissed her on the lips, a long lingering kiss left them both breathless. When Nora pulled away to catch her breath she gasped sorrowfully, 'Tommy you know the next time we meet it might be the last.'

'We better make the most of the time we have then,' Tom said cheekily, trying not to sound too concerned.

Nora responded by pulling Tom closer until their heads were touching.

After what seemed like an age locked in an embrace punctuated by...'Don't go Nora.'

'I don't want to go Tommy.'

'Promise me you'll write,' Tom mumbled when Nora picked up her basket to leave.

Smiling mischievously as she jumped down Nora said.

'There's a chance I might not be going back to England, I'll see you next week.'

Tom fumbled for a reply, taken by surprise at Nora's remark.

'Y-yes hopefully see you next week, Tom Walsh, Knockaun, Ballingar, that's my address just in case I don't see you again.'

Pointing to the cart with her basket, Nora said.

'I know, it's on the side',

Chapter 13

The Priest's House

A nervous glance passed between the boys when they arrived at the priest's house.

Martin looked to Tom for reassurance before lifting the polished brass knocker on the splendidly furnished oak door. After what seemed like an age they heard the sound of heavy bolts being drawn. First the top bolt was drawn, then a pause before they heard the bottom bolt slowly being drawn with clunk as it hit it's stop. Finally a key being turned in a reluctant lock. Tom looked up at the small wooden cross above the door; a silent prayer on his lips as the door began to open. A pair of red-rimmed eyes appeared out of the gloom looking up at them inquiringly. The tired eyes belonged to an old lady dressed entirely in black, the light flooding through the half-opened door emphasised the lines on her face, whom Tom assumed to be the priest's housekeeper.

'The Father is expecting us,' Martin said trying to sound confident.'
'Wait here I'll just.'

Before the old lady could finish, a tall square shouldered man appeared at door, still champing on what Tom assumed...because of the smell of cooking that accompanied him...to be his breakfast. This was the first time Martin had cast his eyes on Father Byrne...Tom had seen him on the street as he passed through the town...for Martin seeing him in the flesh made his reputation more believable.

During his rounds collecting eggs, Tom heard stories about the priest Father Patrick Byrne now standing before them.

Paddy Byrne (as he was known in his youth), a successful prizefighter from Dublin whom at the age of twenty-six 'saw the light' and gave up the chance to earn good money as a boxer and joined the Catholic church.

Paddy's last fight was set up in an old dockside warehouse prepared for fighting by arranging wooden crates to form a large boxing ring.

His opponent on that occasion was a well-known but ageing bare-knuckle boxing champion from the same neighbourhood.

Throughout the fight the pair were evenly matched and seriously hurting each other.

After ten minutes of punishing 'blow for blow' brutality, Paddy delivered right cross that sent the older man crashing to the hard unforgiving floor of the warehouse.

The sound of the opponent's skull hitting the stone slabs would haunt him for the rest of his life.

That was the last punch Paddy Byrne threw as a prizefighter. His opponent, prostrate on the hard floor with his supporters around him, appeared to be close to death.

A priest was called to administer the last rites.

Luckily and to Paddy's relief, his opponent survived, never to fully recover from his horrific head injury and was so severely disabled that he never fought again.

In the days following the fight Paddy turned to the church praying for his opponent's recovery, spending so much time in church praying that a priest was moved to enquire.

'What's troubling you my son?'

Paddy tried to put the priest off by saying,

'I'm fine father. I just need time to think, time alone.'

The wise old the priest could see Paddy was a 'troubled soul'.

Little by little he persuaded the young fighter to confide in him, and took his confession.

After hearing the story of his last fight, he suggested that Paddy might find consolation in doing charitable work around the city. The now ex-boxer soon became a common sight on the streets of Dublin, his warm smile and good humour bringing comfort to the poor and homeless as he distributed food and clothing.

After a year working for the church helping the poor in Dublin, with the priest's recommendation he was accepted into a religious seminary in

Roscommon.

It was the first time Paddy Byrne had been away from Dublin City.

Two years later, to gain field experience Paddy was posted to work alongside a street-wise priest in Galway where he saw at first hand the plight of the poor tenant farmers and their struggle for survival.

His no-nonsense style came to the attention of the Bishop at near-by Tuam.

Within six months he was given the Castlebar posting where his muscular physique and quick wit gave him a reputation as a formidable negotiator with the local population and the Military.

Often the local militia would ask the priest's advice when dealing with disputes between tenants and agents of the absentee landlords, quickly gaining the respect of all.

The imposing figure of Father Byrne filled the doorway wearing a sleeveless cotton vest, a broad leather belt supporting his black ecclesiastical trousers. Unlike any other priest they knew Father Byrne had the appearance of a man that had been in more than a few fights giving away he past life as a bare knuckle boxer. A broken nose, a cauliflower right ear, and biceps like the strong man bending metal bars on Dublin's Grafton Street.

Looking from one to the other the priest greeted the boys with a blessing and asked them to introduce themselves before ushering them to a room at the rear of the house.

Tom's senses took in the musty opulence of the house when the priest led them through to the back room. Expensive looking drapes on the windows, carpets covering most of the stone floor, and quality furniture. A Sacred Heart picture overlooked an oak dining table. In one corner a crucifix above a small alter with two silver candle sticks. Compared to the small three room cottages Tom was familiar with, Father Byrne didn't have much cause for complaint. Probably to keep up appearances and make a good impression when dealing with the ruling classes, Tom thought.

'Would you like a drink'? Father Byrne asked in a surprisingly gentle voice.

'No, no thanks, Father, we're on our way to Westport, Father Quinn told us to call to give you this letter, h-he said you might be able to help me find lodgings in England' Martin answered with a slightly nervous stutter.

The Priest nodded giving little grunts of approval as he read the letter.

Peering over wire-framed spectacles said.

'So one of you is going to England, Liverpool it says here?'

'Yes, I need to find work and somewhere to stay,' Martin answered.

'That's what this letter is about; Father Quinn says you're a good son of the church and a member of the League.

I don't have to tell you what the League is about'.

The old priest paused, his face reddened, his eyes narrowed and with his voice full of passion he banged his fist on the table to emphasise the point and declared.

'Only by being organised, can we stop the evictions, stop the bastards evicting our people. Only by raising funds in can we support our people.'

Tom was taken aback by the strong language coming from a man of god, but thought it was justified under the circumstances.

'Most of our money comes from our friends in America. The big cities like Boston, New York and Chicago are now opening Land League branches with influential Irish patriots donating money. We need to be more active; thousands of our fellow countrymen are sending money home to help their families. That money is now being put to good use by the League to help the evicted families.'

The boys were surprised by the ferocity of the passion in the priest's voice. He finished his tirade by giving them a long knowing stare to let his message sink in until with a soft voice he said.

'Thomas you should think of...'

Before the priest could finish there was a tap-tap on the door and the housekeeper entered to announce,

'Father Fallon from Knockmore to see you Father.'

'Well boys don't forget what I said...good luck in England Martin,' the priest said picking up a neatly folded piece of paper from his desk.

'This is a note of introduction to Father Doyle in Liverpool, he's well respected in the community. When you arrive in Liverpool ask a policeman on the dock for directions to the priest's house. Take Father Doyle's advice, do as he says and you'll be looked after.'

Martin thanked Father Byrne, then just as they were leaving the room Tom noticed a neat pile of foolscap sized papers on the dining table next to the remains of the priest's breakfast; the top sheet had a sketch of a church and was headed, 'From Father Fallon Knockmore'.

Chapter 14

Blight

Two miles out of Castlebar the journey to catch the Steam Packet continued in silence with Martin thinking about an uncertain future in England and Tom thinking about the attractive young girl he had been seeing for the past three weeks. The silence was broken by Martin fidgeting and constantly changing his position on the wooden board that served as a seat.

'Sit still Martin you're making the cart shake.' Tom said, slightly annoyed at having to think of something other than his friendship with Norah Murphy.

'My fekin arse is sore sitting on this fekin wood,' Martin grumbled.
'There's a couple of small potato sacks here in the back, you can sit on them,' Tom said trying to reach them with his free hand.
'If you stop I'll fill them with grass; we can have one each.' Martin said still fidgeting.
'I'll stop just around the next bend, there's a a lot of grass between the trees and the road, it's wide enough to get the cart on.'

Tom stopped the cart on a wide grass verge near a small copse of and ash and elder.
'There's plenty of grass here it'll be dry under the trees.

Tom searched under the trees for dry grass. In a patch of long grass that was raised higher than the surrounding area he came across a makeshift wooden cross with its tip just showing above the grass. Curiosity getting the better of him he decided to take a closer look by clearing the grass from around the cross. Tom had heard from his father of roadside graves from the famine times, usually marked by a simple cross, made by nailing two pieces of wood together. Despite travelling along this road many times this was the first time he'd seen the wooden cross marking what looked like a famine burial.

On cold winter nights with the family gathered around the warm glow of the turf fire, Tom Walsh's father Joe often related stories of his early years.

After living through the misery and depravation of the 'great hunger' Joe constantly warned his children never to forget how the government exported food to England ignoring the plight of the starving millions.

In 1847...during yet another year of potato blight...he remembered a journey he made with his father and twenty other cottiers, (still well enough to make the journey).

Out of desperation, they had decided to walk to Dublin in the hope of a meeting with Government ministers to plead for relief from the dire situation in which they and thousands of their fellow countrymen found themselves.

Along the long and arduous route, they witnessed small groups of starving ragged souls making the long trek across the country to Dublin to catch a boat to Liverpool.

For some walking was almost impossible, having started out bare foot or with poor worn-out footwear, many had their feet bandaged with dirty blood stained rags, hardly able to put one foot in front of the other.

Their few precious belongings in a bundle tied to a stout stick balanced over a weary shoulder, they presented a sorry sight passing through the towns and villages on their tortuous journey of hope.

Many died on the journey before they saw the ship that would take them to a place where they could eat at least one meal a day.

Occasionally, Joe and his fellow travellers would see makeshift wooden crosses at the side of the road, where hurried burials had taken place.

About a mile from Longford, they came across a small crowd of about ten people kneeling in prayer around a mound of freshly dug earth.

Joe and his fellow travellers stopped and doffed their hats in respect.

One of the older mourners walked slowly towards the Ballingar men with his arms outstretched; he thanked them for the thoughtful gesture relating a sad heart rending story of conditions similar to their own.

They had travelled from Bellmullet. After walking for two days many of the party were too exhausted to continue. Like most of the others on the road they were hoping to make it to Dublin and still have enough money for a one-way ticket on the Liverpool steamer.

The nearer Joe and the Ballingar men got to the capital the more fertile fields appeared to be; unlike the dying townships of 'The West' where abandoned houses were becoming a common sight, most of the houses were occupied.

Occasionally people living along the route would come out of their houses with food and water; others turned their backs as if to deny that a problem existed.

Compared to Mayo, life in the Irish Midlands was almost normal.

The people had an air of thriving, not prosperous, but more than just surviving in the midst of the suffering in the less fortunate provinces.

Although they too had lost their potato crop, the fields supported an adequate grain harvest, together with cattle, and sheep; most appeared to be far from starving.

Eventually the travel-weary Ballingar cottiers were at the outskirts of the capital and were joined by other fellow countrymen on the same quest.

After a hurried and patronising meeting with a junior government official spouting a prepared patronising statement, Joe realised that the gruelling effort of journeying across Ireland to see an arrogant civil servant for thirty minutes was a waste of time.

Empty promises.

Soup kitchens, constructing new roads, opening more workhouses.

England has food enough; some of our Irish midland counties are exporting grain.

Are we being forgotten?

Was this a wasted journey?

Little wonder the blighted soil of Eire has seen thousands flee to improve their lot.

These were the thoughts and experiences that Tom's father Joe Walsh related to his family. Stories that Tom would remember for the rest of his life.

When Martin arrived with the potato sacks Tom was still removing the grass from around wooden cross to look for a name to identify the poor soul buried there.

'Who do you thinks buried here,' Tom.

'Don't know, but I remember hearing of a local evicted family with six children living in a Scalp[9] near here during the famine. A family with no other relations to turn to, think they'd all died or emigrated. They intended walking to Dublin, after a few miles the mother and children were too weak to continue, leaving the husband with no option but to dig out a Scalp.

They say that all of the poor starving children died after six weeks of living in those horrendous cold and damp conditions, the parents just gave

---

9   *Scalp, temporary accommodation built over a large hole from materials reclaimed from ruined cottages.*

up, lay down and died in each other's arms, a family wiped out.' Tom said quickly crossing himself.

Chapter 15

Eviction

Tom and Martin were just about to climb onto the cart to continue a more comfortable journey sitting on the grass filled sacks, when they heard the chilling sound of a woman wailing, immediately followed by the cry of children in distress. Martin pointed in the direction of the noise. 'Look, smoke and lots of it, looks like a house on fire.'

'It must be John Mulloy's place, the other side of these trees,' Tom said turning to Martin, 'I collect eggs from there. It's John and Mary Mulloy's place, they live there with their three children they've'...Before he could continue, a gunshot rang out over the trees.

Martin made his way through the bushes keeping low, using the foliage for cover while Tom quickly tethered the donkey following close behind pushing his way through the bushes. With every step closer to the edge of the low shrubbery, the noise coming from the direction of the house of the rose in volume. Shouting, crying, wailing interrupted by a dull thud and the rumble of falling masonry. A few yards ahead Martin dropped onto all fours and signalling Tom to do the same before reaching the edge of the copse where their nostrils caught acrid smell of burning grass and timber.

When the boys raised their heads above the long grass that reaches for light between the bushes they found themselves at the edge of a small field, giving them a clear view of the tragic drama unfolding just a field away. Before them they saw the sad sight of red flames shooting through clouds of black smoke billowing from the grass roof and swirling in the light breeze towards them across the boggy field that lay between them and the house. When the smoke cleared enough to give a clear view of the house they saw the horrifying scene of what remained of the Mulloy cabin still burning, the roof in flames. What was the grass covered roof was almost burned out; charred roof beams had fallen at a crazy angle into the building and were still glowing red as the cruel breeze strove to fan them back to life. Two of the agent's men armed with long iron crowbars were trying to feed the fire by throwing the battered door and window frames onto the flames.

The beleaguered occupants...with the help of friends...had managed to salvage some of their belongings, a table and four chairs, child's crib and a few boxes packed with crockery and other small items, all hurriedly removed and stacked away from the heat.

John Mulloy now passed remonstrating with the agent was pacing up and down looking to the heavens as if hoping for divine intervention. His wife Mary wailing, beside herself with grief. One arm shielding the baby carefully protected by a grey shawl while at the same time trying to comfort their older daughter and son with the other.

The look of horror and disbelief on Mary Mulloy's face with the children clinging to her skirts convinced Tom that here is a cause worth fighting for.

'Look Tom, down there, look soldiers.' Martin whispered pointing

towards the boreen leading to the Mulloy's holding. Twenty yards down the track two of the agent's men protected by three soldiers armed with bayoneted rifles, were loading ladders and what looked like a dismantled battering ram onto a high-sided wagon. Another man was introducing a dishevelled donkey to the shafts of an old turf cart, while another was tying two skeletal looking cattle to the back of the wagon.

'They must have been ready for anything that's a battering ram,' Tom said angrily.

'Yes, like some of the other evictions. Look Tom the feckers, they're taking the old donkey and the cart and the two milking cows,' Martin whispered. 'Yeah, leaving nothing of value, the heartless bastards, now they've no way to move their stuff, everything dumped outside to rot in the weather.' Tom growled angrily.

A small group of neighbours had gathered to witness the eviction. John Mulloy and two of his neighbours were collecting what possessions he had managed to salvage before the heat forced him to watch his home reduced to a shell. His oldest daughter weeping pitifully and now nursing the baby, gently rocking her allowing her mother to pick up what small belongings she could, wrapping them in a patchwork blanket.

Some of the neighbours anxious to help the unfortunate family were... at the orders of the agent...being forced back at bayonet point.

'There's a face to remember,' Tom whispered referring to the agent sitting bolt upright on his horse and judging by the smirk on his face appeared to be enjoying a job well done.

Tom and Martin forgetting Martin had a boat to catch remained concealed in the bushes watching the horrific scene unfold for what seemed like an age, until eventually the red helmeted soldiers escorted the bailiff and his bully-boys away from the burning house down the boreen.
Probably off to evict another unfortunate family, Tom thought..
Just before the landlord's evictors left the scene, his heartless agent swung his horse around and stopped for a moment to admire the destruction, as if to say, that's another one done.

The aftermath of evictions was well known to both Tom and Martin but this was the first time they had witnessed one in progress.
'I know you've a boat to catch but we can't just walk away Martin we must help if we can, let's talk to John Mulloy to see what I can do to help on my way back from the Quay.' Tom suggested.
Both were standing for a better view now that it was safe to do so and were about to break-cover, when Martin noticed something moving in the trees on the opposite side of the field.
'Tom wait, look, there's someone over there, see, over there in the bushes,' Martin whispered gripping Tom's arm to prevent him running from the cover of the trees to talk to John Mulloy.

'There Tom, look over there, someone in the trees at the far edge of the field.'

Two figures were peering from behind the tall bushes on the opposite side of the field; their faces partly covered by the shadow from their hats making it difficult to recognise them. Slowly a tall man emerged from the cover of the trees leading a horse towards the house, followed by the instantly recognisable figure of Mick Fox leading a horse and cart. The boys watched from their viewpoint as the tall man quickly took control helping to load the cart with the salvaged furniture.

'Look Martin it's Mick Fox and the big feller there is Dan Collins, now we know why the smithy's locked,' Tom whispered.
'Yes Dan and Mick are members of the Ballingar branch of the League they must have had word of the eviction,' Martin replied.
It was then that Tom had a flashback to the previous night in Campbell's Bar. It was Dan's arm he saw shaking hands through the curtain. They must have been discussing the Mulloy's eviction.
Realising that the situation was being taken care of, Tom whispered, 'There's nothing we can do here, better be on our way, you've a boat to

catch.'

Chapter 16

Confrontation

After witnessing the cruel heart-rending horror of the Mulloy family eviction, Tom and Martin spent the next half mile of their journey urging the donkey to a faster pace trying to make up lost time, until their attention was attracted by the sound of raised voices.

Tom tugged at Martin's arm and whispered,

'What's that Martin? Listen. Voices coming from over there.' Tom said pointing towards the boreen they were just approaching on their left.

'Listen to the accents. They're not from these parts more like Ulster. That's an Ulster accent.' Martin suggested.

Before they could react three militiamen emerged from a boreen fifteen yards ahead of them. Startled by the sight of the on coming cart, the leader turned his horse to face them signalling the other two to do the same. With all three riders and their horses turned to face them the boys continued forward in anticipation of their next move.

The shortest of the trio gave the others a knowing glance, glance that said let's make life difficult for these two lads. With a nod of his head the three riders took an aggressive stance blocking the road with their horses. Moving slowly in formation towards the cart as if they had done it many times before, forcing Tom to bring the cart to a halt.

Tom instantly took note of the holstered pistols, and rolled his eyes to give Martin a look that said be ready for anything.

The leader, a short stocky man with a permanently curled top lip showing through a grey beard wearing a uniform sporting extra braid on his shoulders, dismounted and strode with a swagger up to the cart, pointed his rifle at them and ordered the them to step down. His two colleagues watched from their high viewpoint, one covering the proceedings with a pistol, the other standing guard watching the road in both directions.

'Better do as they say.' Martin said through gritted teeth.

'What's in these boxes?' Greybeard demanded.

'Eggs, eggs for England,' Tom replied hoping mentioning England would save too thorough a search.

'Open them', Greybeard grunted pointing his bayoneted rifle at the boxes.

'Eggs only eggs, just eggs for England.' Tom repeated shrugging his shoulders.

Greybeard cocked his rifle and demanded again.

'Open the boxes or we'll smash them open.'

'All the boxes open. And that,' Greybeard ordered pointing to Martin's bag.

Tom and Martin proceeded to unload the boxes, leaving three on the cart.

Finding only eggs in the crates on the road Greybeard was about to turn his attention to the cart and Martin's bag when a soldier arrived from the direction of Westport. After taking note of the scene he shouted in a loud commanding voice for all to hear.

'We've been ordered to the docks, there's a French coaster coming in, it's due to dock in the next hour leave those two for now. We searched that cart last week and found nothing.'

When the soldiers were out of earshot, Tom said. 'That one, the one who called those other three feckers away to the docks, stopped me last week. Did you hear his accent he sounded English? He said they're working with the Constabulary. Luckily it was just a quick check with no eggs broken,'

'Come on Tom, let's get these crates back on the cart and no more stops we should be in Westport by now, hurry or we wont have time for a farewell drink at Matt Kelly's,' Martin chided impatiently.

Chapter 17

Nora's Secret

Four days earlier.
Tom realised that if Nora Murphy were to return to England within the next two weeks on the Steam Packet from Westport, it would most likely be on the same day as Martin.

I have to persuade her to stay at the farm. I know she wants to stay. She likes living here and gets on well with her auntie. Her auntie needs her. Tom thought while carefully loading the crates packed with fresh eggs for another run to the Westport.

Tom's confidence in their relationship had grown at every meeting; they had an understanding he convinced himself. Nora was the girl for him and he wanted to tell her so.

By now the lovelorn pair had timed their meeting at the junction of the road and the boreen almost perfectly. On the last occasion Tom and Nora met, Nora accepted a ride into town as if it was the normal thing to do, making herself as comfortable as possible on the hard board which served as a seat whilst still keeping a respectable distance then turned to Tom and said quietly,

'Tom I've got something to tell you.'

But for the wicked smile lighting Nora's face, a girl saying that would have worried him.

Before Tom had chance to ask what she had to tell him Nora reassured him.

'My auntie's can't see very well and not very good at writing and since I've been here she asks me to write her letters and help her with her money, paying bills and stuff, well.' Nora paused, teasingly looking into Tom's eyes.

' Well a few days after we first met, she asked me to write to my da on her behalf saying what a good help I was and that she would find it very hard to manage without me, and could I stay for a few more weeks. I laid it on a bit thick ya know although it's true, she's does find it hard work on her own. I put in the letter that Auntie needed help to look after the farm. Even though there's only the chickens and a couple of milking cows, it's a hard for an old lady on her own.'

Tom thought for a few seconds.

'You must like it here, I mean er, er, would you like to stay here always, you know, live with your aunt and settle down here?' he stuttered.

'It's not up to me, it's me ma and da, their house in England is small, its in a crowded back court, two small bedrooms and with all me brothers…four, I'm the only girl…it might suit them better for me to stay here with auntie.' Nora said trying to look serious whilst smiling at the same time.

'We've not had a reply yet Tom, and if a letter doesn't arrive soon, I might be on the same boat as your friend Martin, Nora said sounding less optimistic .

'Your saying this might be the last time we see each other, better make the most of it,' Tom said with a cheeky smile.

'Don't get any ideas Mr Walsh I'm a good catholic girl, you know what I mean,' pointing to her vacant ring finger.

'Sorry, sorry, I meant time for us to talk and be together,' Tom flushed trying to regain his composure.

'Don't worry Tommy I know exactly what you mean, I don't want to go back to England, I like it here living with auntie, I want to stay here with you.' Nora said touching his hand to emphasise her point.

'No one calls me Tommy, me ma calls me Thomas, I like the way you say it Nora.'

Tom said turning to concentrate on the steep incline.

'From now on I'll call you Tommy, Tommy Walsh,' she said touching his free hand again adding. 'There's another good reason why I might be able stay longer, perhaps longer than you think.'

Trying to hide the excitement in this voice Tom said, 'What reason is that Nora Murphy,'

Putting on her most serious voice Nora continued.

'I can't say until after I get the letter from me Ma and Da. It depends what they have to say. Then I have to think what I want to do.' Nora said, trying not to smile while looking straight ahead.

'Why the mystery, you can tell me, don't keep me guessing' Tom pleaded stopping the cart at the bakery.

'It's to do with the farm that's all I can say,' Nora teased stepping down giving Tom's hand an extra tight squeeze leaving him a little perplexed and smiling to himself as he continued on his way trying to guess what Nora's secret might be.

Chapter 18

Westport Quay

At the top of a long winding hill, Tom and Martin looked down onto the town of Westport with earth scented smoke curling upwards from the rooftops and beyond the town was the beautiful panorama of Clew Bay.

Seeing the town and the quay where the steamer would be docked caused Martin's stomach to churn with mixed emotions.

The reality of what he was leaving behind. His friends, family and his home town of Ballingar where almost everyone is a friend or a friend of the family. Still, with very little work to be found here, he convinced himself, he was doing the right thing, that his future was elsewhere, others had left home and made a success of it.

Tom also had mixed emotions too, he could be losing his best friend and his beloved Nora on the same day. Four days had passed since she told him she might be going home, this could be his last chance to see her. Will she be on her way to town for bread or at the Quay catching the boat to Liverpool? What was the secret she hinted at when they last met?

'She's not here then,' Martin said, waking Tom from his romantic thoughts when they passed the Murphy farm.

Martin heard about Tom's friend Nora in Campbell's bar after copious jars of ale loosened Tom's tongue; and was eager to see the girl Tom enthused about before leaving for England.

'We might see her in the town' Tom said; trying not to sound too disappointed.

'Is this the bread shop she goes to?' Martin asked a few minutes later when they arrived at the bakery.

'Won't be a minute,' Tom mumbled pretending he hadn't heard the question.

A couple of minutes later he emerged sad-faced with a halfpenny bun on the pretext it might cure his 'queasy stomach'.

Westport Quay was busier than usual. Two Coasters one French and one English in the process of unloading. A four- master anchored out in the bay waiting for a berth and the Steam Packet berthed at the far end of the quay with black smoke spiralling across the bay from her funnel as stokers strived to raise a good head of steam in readiness for the long journey north around Ireland's Atlantic coast. From the gangplank a long queue of weary looking passengers waiting to board meandered around the stacks of wooden cases and other cargo deposited on the quay.

It took all of Tom's concentration to thread the cart loaded with eggs along the bustling Quay, through cargo being unloading directly onto wagons, their horses feeding from nosebags to give them the energy to haul the heavy load.

Even though Tom had seen the migrant families many times at the quay, it always made a sorry sight to see his fellow country-folk forced to escape the hardship and pandemonium caused in the wake of rent racking and evictions.

Mothers, comforting malnourished children clinging to their skirts whilst holding hungry babies to their breasts. Older children playing amongst the cargo, climbing on boxes waiting to be loaded, parents with baggage at their feet, their patience tried to the limit trying to keep their children in order.

Tom was saddened to see every generation represented, from the new-born babe in arms to the aged grand parents making the journey to a new life, afraid of being left alone in their later years.

Chapter 19

Ned 'O' Malley Exporter

Ned 'O' Malley's yard is set close to the back wall of Westport quay, alongside a long row of warehouses. To the rear is a compound for loading and unloading goods for export with a gate to enter and another to leave. Over the main entrance gate is a roughly hand painted sign proclaiming, *'EDWARD O MALLEY EXPORTER'*.

Tom could see three large four wheel carts waiting to be off-loaded as they approached the yard. Good, he thought, this gives me time to search the quay for Nora to see whether she's booked on the same boat as Martin.

'She's not here, perhaps she's already gone,' Tom said to Martin once he'd established that she wasn't in the queue for the steamer.

'Don't think so, there's been no other sailing for two weeks this is the only one, the only other sailing is from Dublin and I don't think she'd want to travel all the way across the country when she can sail from here. There's nothing you can do now Tom if she's gone you'll have to wait for a letter, anyway I'd better be looking for our Paddy,' Martin said sounding a little impatient.

Martin's cousin Paddy Gallagher works on the docks. When he and Martin last met, Martin promised to have a farewell drink before leaving for England.

'OK I'll come with you; It'll be a while before Ned's lad checks me in.' Tom replied with a sigh of resignation-thinking about Nora.

'Still carting eggs Tom? Thought you would be going away by now like our Martin,' Paddy teased after they found him a few yards farther along the quay with a stick in each hand, herding cattle onto one of the coasters. .

Before Tom could answer Paddy continued.

'How about a quick jar Tom, a farewell drink for Martin, the steamer doesn't sail for another hour at least.'

'I'll join you two when I've settled with Ned 'O Malley,' Tom said, making an excuse to search for Nora again, leaving Martin and Paddy heading for Matt Kelly's bar.

Tom did a quick search of the quay, again searching the queue and the small wooden booking office without a sight of the girl that was by now a lot more than a friend.

When he arrived a little breathless at the exporters yard Tom found one of Ned's young assistants leading the donkey and the empty cart to the rear of the compound.

'She'll be safe here Tom, the boss's said to call in the office for the money,' the youth assured Tom knowing he liked to visit the pub before making the journey home.

Chapter 20

Matt Kelly's Bar

Matt Kelly's bar is the favourite quayside bar for migratory men to have their last drink of anything Irish before leaving their homeland for a new life.

Unmarried and married men travelling alone tend to gather in the back room, while the married men travelling with their family's prefer to drink near to the door where they can keep an eye on them standing in the queue waiting to board the steamer.

The front room is sectioned off into three areas. Near to the entrance a small all standing area with shoulder height shelves around the walls. The mid section is furnished with makeshift stools and ledges to rest tankards, maximising the floor space with more people standing than sitting. Cast iron tables with oak tops, now almost black with years of use, line the small rear area of the front room either side of open double doors to the back room.

The back room has four long pine tables with benches for seats set on an uneven stone floor. Set in the back corner is a shallow arched fireplace with an ever glowing turf fire, alongside a small raised wooden platform where local musicians come to entertain for little or no remuneration, sometimes just for free beer.

The odorous fusion of ale, tobacco, and smouldering turf greeted Tom long before he crossed the threshold of the busy hostelry. Tom carefully navigated his way through the packed bar, obliged to make silent apologies for pushing past men holding jars of ale face to face deep in conversation. Squinting to see through stinging eyes, caused by the smoke-laden atmosphere hanging like a dark blue cloud under the low ceiling he headed for the back room. Tom noticed two men dressed in black great coats hunched over a table near the doorway, their heads almost touching as if not wanting to be heard. Ulster men for sure Tom concluded, better tread carefully he thought before entering the dimly lit back room. Tom peered through the smoky haze scanning the tables looking for Martin and Paddy. A pair of guttered candles on a wrought iron bracket supplemented the little light that entered the crowded space through a small grubby single pane window. The room was buzzing with the chatter of men waiting to embark on the journey of a lifetime, a journey of hope. For most a journey that…apart from hearsay from friends and letters from relatives…was a journey to the unknown filled with apprehension.

Next to a smoke stained fireplace where the turf fire seemed to burn forever without any apparent attention, a toothless fiddler with a face as red as the glowing turf was in conversation with one the migrants.

He looks very much like the fiddler in Ballingar market or perhaps they all looked like that, Tom thought.

Tom eased himself alongside Martin on the bench seat, picked up the jar of ale that Martin had got in for him and as if he was about to make a speech and proclaimed,' Cheers Martin.' Before he could continue to say how he was going to miss his friend and wish him safe journey, the fiddler started plying his trade filling the room with the sound of the latest popular jig.

'Ready for another,' Paddy mouthed pointing to Martins empty tankard. 'No thanks better not miss the Packet,' Martin mouthed back.

Once outside in the fresh air, Tom whispered, 'Did you see those two in black coats, from the north, they think we don't know, their accent gives them away.'   'They're always here checking the ships for firearms, been here most of the day, they check every ship as it docks,' Paddy complained.

Chapter 21

Boarding the Steam Packet

'Come on lads, hurry, the sooner I get on that ship the better,' Martin said anxiously turning to look towards the Steam Packet and almost walking into a stack of bales as the trio made their way through the cargo stacked along the busy quay. 'Don't worry there's plenty of time, it has to wait for the tide to turn,' Paddy reassured Martin.

Suddenly, just as they rounded a stack of flax bales. 'Look, look Tom, aren't those the two feckers that stopped us.' Martin whispered anxiously, pointing to a coaster anchored next to the Steam Packet.

'It's Greybeard again, and his two mates, looks like they're searching the cargo as it's unloaded' Tom whispered.

'Searching for guns and contraband; their Sargent checks the tide-tables and sends a squad here before they dock, the feckers are everywhere. Up and down the coast looking for boats offloading onto smaller ones that can run onto the beach,' Paddy snarled.

'Come on lets get onboard before those feckers stop us again,' Tom urged.

'Oh no, look at that queue,' Martin said wearily pointing to the four deep queue of migrants still waiting to board the steamer.

'Grab one of those boxes, they'll think you're working with me,' Paddy whispered with a sideways nod at small wooden crates waiting to be loaded.

Following Paddy's lead Tom and Martin each carried one of the small crates up the gangplank marked 'crew only.'

'Not so fast,' Martin gasped, struggling with his bag trapped between his chest and the crate.

In the comparative safety of the ship's hold, Tom turned to Martin and shook his hand, realising he might not see his best friend again said, 'Don't forget to write to us and to your ma and da.'

'I will Tom and I'll be coming back when I have the funds. Got to find a job first,' Martin choked starting to feel the emotion of the occasion.

'Watch out for those English girls,' Paddy chided trying to lighten the mood, his hands outlining shape of the female form before shaking Martin's hand.

After a a few seconds of silence Paddy turned to Tom and said, 'we'd better go I'm finished here on the dock for today, you can give me a ride into town, best of luck in England Martin, write to me if you have time.'

'What a day Paddy,' Tom said with a sigh as they made their way down the gangplank. Suddenly Tom stopped and nudged Paddy and said quietly, 'Look, look, see those two characters leaning against the wall on the far side of the quay.

'The two from the bar' Paddy whispered behind his hand.

'We don't need any more trouble, do we have to pass them to get to the cart?' Tom asked thinking about looking for Nora on the way.

'No, follow me, we can go around the back to Ned's yard,' Paddy said pointing to a narrow passageway between the warehouses.

Chapter 22

An Assault

So as not to attract too much attention from the military, Tom and Paddy strolled casually across the quay to the warehouses lining the back of the quayside, quietly slipping into the dimly lit passageway. They walked slowly, their eyes squinting to adjust to the semi darkness then stopped when they heard a man's voice raised in anger, swearing and shouting obscenities followed by the muffled cries of help from a female voice. Tom tapped Paddy on the shoulder simultaneously signalling to be quiet, pointing towards the back of the warehouse. Without saying a word they ran the few yards to the back of the building where they saw a young girl pinned against the wall by a great-coated man trying to lift her skirts with one hand while covering her mouth with the other.

Preoccupied and unaware of their presence the man continued his brutal attack, swearing through gritted teeth,

'Irish bitch be still or you'll be sorry.'

The poor girl looked exhausted, with very little resistance left.

The attacker so intent on ravishing the distressed girl that he was oblivious to his surroundings and didn't hear Tom and Paddy approaching from behind.

Tom reacted first pulling the attacker away from the struggling girl by grabbing the great-coat's conveniently large collar. As the man spun around Paddy took a mighty right hand swing landing mid belly doubling him up. Instinctively Tom kneed his chin as he bent double laying the attacker out flat then moved in quickly to finish him off until he noticed blood coming from a cut on the man's head.

'Must have been when his head hit the floor,' Martin said.

Tom checked the man for signs of life, as there was no movement from the man now lying prostrate before them.

'He's still alive just out cold, that'll teach English Agents to mess with Irish girls,' Tom said turning to the girl they'd just saved.

'Yes, oh thank you, thank you so much, that man he...' the girl sobbed hurriedly tidying her skirts.

Paddy picked up a shawl and the drawstring purse the distressed girl had dropped during the struggle.

'Are you hurt, are you OK,' Paddy enquired in his most sympathetic voice placing the shawl gently around the girl's shoulders.

'I'm all right now thank you, I have to go my ma will be waiting for me, I was on my way home when that man came and walked alongside me as if he was with me.

Before I could call for help he pushed me down the this alley,' the girl explained between sobs.

'Come on I'll walk with you to make sure your safe. Tom, you take care of this one before he comes round, I'll meet you at Ned's yard, Paddy said taking charge of the situation.

Paddy returned to the yard to find Tom sitting on the cart talking to Ned's young assistant.

'Let's get away from this place before there's any more trouble,' Tom said rattling the reins to encourage the donkey to make haste.

'What did you do with that English fecker? Hope you took good care of him, don't want him coming after us,' Paddy asked as they left the quay.

'I was going to clobber him again but he was still out cold so I propped him against the wall, put an empty ale bottle I found nearby by his hand and wasted no time getting here.' Tom replied, with a hint of a smile.

'And what about that poor girl Paddy, she looked badly shaken?' Tom enquired.

'I walked with her to the end of the quay where it was busy enough for her to walk home in safety.' Paddy said with a cheeky smile lighting his face.

'What did you find out about her, did she tell you why she was at the quay by herself?'

Tom asked curious to know why Paddy was smiling.

'She was there to see her sister 'off' to England on the Steamer, her sister's joining her husband now that he has a job and lodgings. I got her name, her age and where she lives,' Paddy grinned.

'Tell me then, how old is she? I would say about seventeen, it was hard to tell through the tears, I could see she's a good-looker.'

'You're wrong about her age she's eighteen almost nineteen.

Her name's Anne and lives with her parents on the Newport road the other side of town. She said she's thinking of going to England to look for a job. When I said we might see each other again she said that would be nice. Paddy said with a smile as wide as the bay.

Then I asked about that fella that attacked her and is she going to report it to the Garda? She said not, in case they pull us two in for assault...you know how they twist things...can't trust em,' Paddy added in a more serious tone.

'I'll look out for you next time I'm down here at the quay, you might have more news to tell me about the girl Anne,' Tom said nudging Paddy.

'Thanks for the ride this is where I get off,' Paddy said offering Tom his hand.

For the last few minutes Tom had been scanning the streets peering into windows and open doorways of the shops in the hope of seeing Nora, and had almost forgotten Paddy was sitting next to him.

Tom stopped the cart and sighed. 'Well Paddy it's been great seeing you again, it's been quite a day, different in many ways. Your Martin on his way to England, don't know when we'll see him again, if ever. Don't know where my friend Nora is, she might have gone as well. On the way here we saw the Mulloy family being evicted and their house taken down,' Tom stopped short on mentioning the League, best not, he thought.

'And that fiasco in the alley,' Paddy reminded jumping down from the cart.

'Next time we'll have a few more jars,' Paddy shouted before disappearing into the nearest bar.

Chapter 23

Good News

Alone with his thoughts of the day's events, Tom walked up the hill leading the donkey as he always does on his way home from the docks. When he arrived at the bakery Tom could see the shop was empty and with the aroma of fresh baking beckoning him in, he couldn't resist the temptation to buy a bun.

'Aren't you the friend of the girl Nora,' the buxom lady behind the counter said handing Tom a freshly baked bun.

Tom's faced flushed as he handed over a penny. 'Yes have you seen her today.'

'You've just missed her, she'll be on her way home,' she answered, a knowing smile lighting her face.

Seconds later Tom was almost dragging the donkey up the hill stopping every few yards to stand on the cart...his hand shading his eyes like a sailor looking out to sea...searching for Nora among the commuters travelling to and from the town. After standing on the cart for the third time, he spotted a figure with auburn hair escaping from a plaid shawl near the top of the incline.

She still here, she's not going to England, I can catch her up if I run, Tom thought clutching the halter as if his life depended on it.

He soon realised running up the hill whist trying to drag a donkey and cart was out of the question and quickly reverted to a more dignified hurried walk.

Within minutes, he could see that he was making ground on the girl.

It is her I can see the wicker basket.

'NORA, NORA,' Tom shouted impatiently though cupped hands, hoping she would hear from five hundred yards.

With no reaction...apart for the passers by looking at him...and on almost level ground he jumped on the cart and rattled the reins on the donkey's back encouraging it to a more urgent pace.' Still gaining, now at three hundred yards, he shouted again, this time Nora stopped, turned to see Tom standing on the cart. With a smile and a wave she picked up her skirts and started to run towards him, her shawl falling to her shoulders allowing her auburn hair to flow like a tail of fire in the breeze.

Spurred on by the sight of the broad smile lighting Nora's face Tom again encouraged the donkey to hurry so much it was trotting like a pony, causing the empty egg boxes to rattle about on the back of the cart.

Disregarding the custom and the passers by, Nora fell into Tom's welcoming arms until she was gasping from the strength of his embrace.

'I'm so happy you are still here,' Tom whispered releasing Nora from his vice like grip.

Still catching her breath Nora turned to Tom and in a low serious voice said.

'Thomas Walsh I have good news to announce.'

'And what might that be Nora Murphy,' Tom returned mimicking the same tone.

They looked at each other and laughed as Tom demanded,

'Come on, come on tell me the news, don't tease.'

'A letter arrived yesterday from my mother, she says I can stay with my Aunt as long as she needs me.'

Before Nora could continue, Tom held her hand, looked into her eyes and whispered, 'That's the news I've been hoping for Nora'.

Nora took her usual place on the cart, this time she moved closer allowing her skirt to brush against Tom's leg.

'There's other things in the letter too Tommy Walsh, I'll tell you the rest on the way,' Nora said edging closer.

The letter from Nora's mother contained the good news that Tom was hoping for, and more.
Their small rented house in England, was already over crowded and with another baby on the way it would help their situation if Nora could stay with her aunt at the farm.

Nora's mother realised that her sister-in-law (Nora's aunt) not having any family had grown fond of her niece regarding her as the daughter she never had, and would be glad of the help and companionship that Nora could provide while living with her.

Tom arrived home at Knockaun later that evening to find that the boreen had dried, exposing the holes that caused the boxes to fall off the cart, reminding him of the day, the day that in the end was not such a bad day after all. Nora was staying to live with her aunt, Martin was in time to catch the steamer, the Mulloy's were evicted and were looked after by the Land League, and he and Paddy saved a pretty girl from an assault.

The day was better than he could have hoped, it was, a day that was different.

Chapter 24

Flashbacks

Mon 10/3/1879

On a welcome day off from collecting eggs Tom was assisting his brother Mick load a cart of dry turf to be delivered to the Priest's house in Ballingar and was having difficulty concentrating on the work in hand.

A week had past since the day of Martin's departure on the steam packet to England. As well as missing his best friend Martin and thinking about his future with Nora, Tom's mind kept wandering to the scene of the eviction he witnessed the previous week.

Random flashbacks...vivid pictures of the horrific eviction of the Mulloy's.

The weeping mother.

The look of horror on the children's faces as they clung to her skirts.

The self-satisfied look on the agent's face when overlooking the demolition.

The smoke seeping through the grass thatch on the roof, still damp from the recent rain. Flames fanned by the breeze suddenly taking hold, leaping like ghostly sprites trying to escape through the grey-white smoke. The broken door hanging forlornly on one hinge after submitting to the unequal strength of the mighty battering ram.

These images disturbed Tom in the days and nights following the cruel eviction of the Mulloy family, possessing his thoughts at the most unexpected times.

How many more families are to suffer this fate?

How many more families will be forced take shelter in the workhouse or sleep-rough in the hedgerows or be split up to lodge with friends and relatives?

How can I help?

My friends, my neighbours are all at risk due to the greed of the landlords. Landlords that don't belong here. They don't live here, most live in England, yet they have the means to ruin our lives.

We'll get justice one day.

'Come on Tom put your back into it,' Mick chided while loading the high-sided donkey cart that they had drawn up alongside the lean-to turf shed.

Working with his brother reminded Tom of what Martin had related about the League a week before, and was keen to learn more from Mick.

He decided on the direct approach.

'The League Mick, the Land League what is it about?' Tom enquired tentatively.

Tom had heard Martin's account of the League's cause in helping the evicted tenants and opposing rent racking, now he was curious to hear his brother's explanation of its aims and how it will help stop the evictions.

Mick turned and looked at Tom through half- closed eyes and a hint of a smile.

'Who told you about The League?'

'I've always known about The League, but not really thought much about it till I saw the Mulloys being thrown off their land and heard you are a member.

Tom went on to relate what he and Martin had seen at the Mulloy house, and that Martin told him how the League was trying to stop the evictions.

'Everyone knows about the evictions and about not co-operating with the English fecker in the 'Big House'; that was the first time I saw for myself a family being evicted. It shocked me Mick, to see Mulloy his wife, his children and all their stuff thrown out of the house. They set light to it, reduced it to rubble.

That family had lived on that land for generations; we have to do something Mick. I told Martin I would join the Land League in his place now he's gone to England.'

After a short pause Mick looked at his brother nodded his head and said. 'We have a League committee in town if you are serious about joining you can come with me to the next meeting, you'll know most of the members and will like what we are doing to help our people.'

'Now let's get on and deliver this load, then you can do your run to Westport. Talking of Westport how's your friend Martin doin in England.'

'To soon for a letter Mick, hope he's found somewhere to stay,' Tom replied throwing the last of the turf to his brother.

Chapter 25

Martin on Merseyside

Sat 8/3/1879

'Is that Liverpool? Martin inquired of a deckhand busy oiling a nearby winch. 'No lad that's a village called Formby. Liverpool is over there where those big chimneys are, see the smoke, we'll be there in less than an hour.' The man replied pointing to swirling plumes of black smoke from what looked like hundreds of very tall chimneys the like of which Martin had never seen before.

'You'll soon see when we sail up the river, look, there's the mouth of the river in the distance, it's called the Mersey, the river Mersey' he said pointing with his oilcan.

Twenty minutes later Martin was leaning on the deck rail looking in wonder at the densely built up city getting closer as the steamer slowly made it's way up the river. Martin preferred to be on deck, not just to see the city of Liverpool for the first time, but to get some fresh air. Happy to brave the cold wind to get way from the stench of vomit and other bodily odours that pervaded the lower decks after the long and at times nauseous voyage around the coast of Ireland and into the Irish Sea.

The buildings seemed to get bigger the closer they got to the city, closing in on him, intimidating.

The air around him changed. No longer the salty ozone of sea air, it smelled different you could almost taste it.

I don't think you could grow anything here in this air it wouldn't survive, not like home in Mayo, Martin thought watching the endless river traffic. Ships of all sizes sailing to and from the port their wakes merging and crossing each other causing smaller boats at anchor to bob up and down like jockeys at Ballinrobe races.

'Father Byrne said when you get off the boat, find a policeman ,' Martin mumbled under his breath while pushing his way along the crowded Liverpool quay, avoiding a clanking steam crane unloading cotton bales whilst trying to read Father Doyle's address scribbled on the now crumpled piece of paper Father Byrne had given him.

'You're on the wrong side of the water lad, you'll have to take the ferry. Over there further along the quay, that's the ticket office for the Ferry across the river to Birkenhead, ask again on the other side.' The policeman said sounding friendlier than he looked with the black and gold night stick hanging from his belt.

'FERRY TO BIRKENHEAD' the notice proclaimed above the door on the wooden ticket office.

Fifteen minutes later on the Birkenhead side of the river, Martin was stepping off the ferry onto the floating landing stage where the wash of passing river traffic caused it to rise and fall, making the walk onto the Woodside Quay like rolling home after too much ale.

So this is Birkenhead, I thought it was all Liverpool. Martin mumbled to himself looking around for a Policeman on the crowded Quay at the same time fumbling in his coat pocket for the paper with the Priest's address.

Whilst preoccupied searching his pockets, a lady dressed different to any female Martin had seen before...her red and black dress with lace frilled hem showing more ankle than was modest...accosted him.

'Can I help you young man she said smiling through the longest eyelashes he'd ever seen.

'Err, Err, I'm looking for a policeman,' he stuttered,

'I'm trying to avoid them, they just try to stop me making an honest living, if you've got money I can show you a good time,' she proposed, through bright red lips that seemed to dominate her face.

Remembering the advice of his father during a quiet father-son conversation Martin realised what this lady was offering and hastily responded with, 'Thanks for your offer Miss but I must find the priest's house, I'm told a policeman will tell me the way.'

'Ask at the gate over there there's usually a bobby checking goods and stuff,' she said in a disappointed tone, 'are you sure you don't want good time,' she tried again.

'No thanks and thanks for the information,' Martin shouted over his shoulder heading in the direction the lady had pointed in search of the gate.

The policeman on gate duty pointed to an old man with a besom and shovel, picking up horse droppings from the cobbled road.

'Ask him over there, he goes to mass on Sundays. I've no idea where the priest lives, no time for em I go to the chapel,' he said abruptly.

'You're not the first to ask me that question,' the old road sweeper replied in a soft brogue that gave away his west of Ireland roots reminding

Martin of home.

'The answers always the same, follow this road until you come to a square on Grange road.

The big church is the one you want St Werburgh's with a big house next to it, that's the priest's house.

Tell the Father, Paddy from the docks sent ya an he'll treat you well; with your accent he would anyhow,' he laughed as he emptied the contents of his shovel into a wooden wheelbarrow.

Chapter 26

Martin's deal with the Priest

The red sandstone church was easier to find than a way to the priest's house. Martin could see what he thought could be the priest's house next to the church within the church grounds. The way to the house wasn't immediately obvious until he noticed an old iron gate set in a sandstone arch with the name Werburgh above Roman numerals.

Martin stood looking at the iron gate collecting his thoughts trying to remember what he would say to the priest or to just hand him the letter from Father Byrne. After pushing it open and walking slowly along a stone path he found himself looking at an imposing dark oak front door furnished with a polished brass knocker cast in the shape of a fox. Martin stood looking at the door nervously gathering his courage. I've come this far and I need somewhere to live I have no other choice he convinced himself lifting the head of the fox.

'I've got this letter from Father Byrne, he said to show it to Father Doyle' Martin said meekly to the rather large lady answering the door.

'Wait there,' she commanded causing the lad an involuntary shiver, then changed her mind adding, 'No no, better follow me,' showing the young Irishman along a tiled hallway to a musty smelling room what Martin took to be the priest's office.

'The Father's in prayers, take a seat by the window, he'll be here in a few minutes,' she said in a tone that was not to be questioned before closing the door.

Sitting by the window taking in the opulence of the well furnished room, Martin could see how the catholic church in England looks after it's priests. The leather upholstered couches placed either side of the bay window, the tall well stocked bookcase and the thick piled carpet with Chinese dragons around it's border covered most of the dark stained oak floorboards.

Five minutes later Martin was awakened from his thoughts when the priest with his black and gold cassock brushing the carpet entered the room placing a large leather bound bible on the table, and said in a loud voice.

'Hello young man, I'm Father Doyle how can I help you? what's your name?'

'Martin Cassidy, Father, I have this letter from Father Byrne in Castlebar he said to come to see you.' Martin said handing a crumpled envelope to the priest.

'Yes Martin I know things are bad over there, I receive one of these letters from over the water almost every week and the answer is the same, we have things to discuss before I can say, welcome to my church. I see you're a member of the Land League and from an evicted family,' the priest said looking over his half spectacles as if waiting far a reply.

'It say that in the letter?' Martin puzzled.

'Yes it says your family were evicted but nothing about the League, see here these two letters in the corner LL that tells me you are a member of the Land League and to look after you.

The priest turned in his chair to face the young Irishman and said in a more serious voice.

'Now let's see what we can do for you. This is how it works.

There are three main groups of workers employed in most of the big factories and boatyards on this river. There's the men put in and looked after by the Masons, the ones put in by us the Roman Church and then there's the rest, the ordinary folk with no loyalty to any organisation apart from a small number of Protestants, it's all about who you know and who will look after your interests in this town.'

'I've heard of Protestants but Masons don't they build the churches? Martin interrupted.

'No no, they're an ancient secret organisation that look after their members and their families, a bit like what I'm offering you, you'll find out soon enough,' the priest said turning to his bookcase and picking out two small ledgers secreted behind a shelf of large leather bound volumes.

'These are the two most important books in this room, one contains a list of workplaces where our people employed, the other has a list of houses where you can find safe board and lodging for a reasonable sum with a good catholic family.

Follow the rules of the church...my rules...and you'll be looked after, for this I expect you to be loyal and generous to us, the church, take another path and there will be consequences.'

'I will help and come to mass but how can I be generous I don't understand?' Martin asked looking slightly puzzled.

'As I said you will be looked after in many ways as you will find out. You can be generous by giving a small percentage of your wages to the church, it will be collected every Sunday morning at eleven-o-clock mass. If you miss a mass you can put the money aside to pay double the following week.' The priest said calmly with a smile that said you will do as I say if you know what's good for you.

'Now first we must find somewhere for you to stay,' thumbing through the ledger marked ADDRESSES.

'Here is the name and address of a good catholic family. Jim Grogan is the head of the family, a good man, tell him I sent you and he'll give you a bed and board, you can make your own arrangements with him regarding rent.

The Birkenhead Iron Works is where you will be employed Jim Grogan will take you there and introduce you to the man in charge, he's another one of ours' the priest said copying the information on a sheet of parish notepaper.

'Thank you for your help Father,' Martin said as he turned to go.

'Wait, I'll walk with you to the end of the road to show you the way, it's easy to get lost in a strange town.'

Chapter 27

Nora's Inheritance

Tom saw Nora twice during the week following Martin's departure. On the second occasion just as they were about to part she surprised him holding his hand and saying, 'My aunt would like you to call at the farm next week on your way home from the Quay so best if you don't call in Matt Kelly's for a drink.'

Before Tom could answer, Nora blushed, 'She knows all about us...you know what I mean, us walking out...and would like to meet you.'

Tom looked at Nora for a few seconds hoping of more information, before answering apprehensively. 'Yes I'll call next Tuesday on my way home, meet me at the usual place.'

When Tuesday morning arrived it was one of those spring mornings that make you feel good to be alive, the air was fresh and the birds seemed to sing louder than ever. A mist capped the holy mountain, rolling down the side facing the bay like a glistening silver cape.

Tom never noticed the beautiful day or his surroundings. Meeting Nora's aunt for what he assumed was an informal chat occupied his thoughts that morning from the moment he opened his eyes.

'What's it about? Why does she want to see me?' Tom asked Nora when they met at the end of the boreen.

Tom's questions went unanswered apart from, 'You'll see, you'll be surprised,' Nora said trying to sound serious behind a wicked smile when the house came into sight.

'Come on in Tommy don't worry,' Nora teased, lifting her skirts clear of the stone floor. Tom followed close behind, into the warm homely aroma of food being cooked .

'Hello you must be Tom I've heard a lot about you from Nora, it's Tom this and Tom that, now you're here can I offer you a drink?'

The old lady said pointing with one hand to the teapot at the side of the fire while stirring a pot of stew with the other.

'I'll get it,' Nora said before Tom could answer.

'I bet a growing lad like you could eat some stew, stay for dinner Tom then we'll have a chat,' Mrs Murphy said in a voice that was difficult to refuse.

'Now Thomas,' Mrs Murphy said looking Tom in the eye causing him to react with an embarrassed nod. 'Nora has most likely told you I have no one in my family to take over this farm... apart from John, Nora's father...now that my Billy has 'passed on' and John's not interested in coming home to work the farm now he's settled in England. I can tell you in confidence that I am seriously considering leaving the farm to Nora all of it, the farm and the land, but there are conditions, conditions that are not too harsh or too difficult to keep.

First and most importantly, I will live here and own the farm jointly with Nora and her husband until I pass on.

Second, Nora must be able to run and maintain the farm which means she must have a husband.

Third, Nora can choose who she marries but I must approve as he will be living in my house.

Those are my conditions. What do you think Thomas?' Mrs Murphy said looking at Tom then turning to Nora as if for approval.

Tom, taken aback by what he had just heard could only say, 'I didn't know you owned the farm Mrs Murphy.'

'Yes, yes I do own the farm Thomas, I hold the deeds to the house and the land.   Now that we've got an understanding.'

'Please call me Tom Mrs Murphy,' Tom interrupted.

Ignoring Tom's interruption Mrs Murphy continued, 'I'll tell you both in strictest confidence how I came to own this farm.'

Chapter 28

Bridie Murphy's story

'When I was a young girl...Bridie Keene before I married Billy Murphy...I was a maid for the Marquis at the big house in the town, you know, the one by the Quay.

Well the son of the old Marquis Mr Boyle, him that owns it and all this land around here asked me to look after his father, to be his personal maid when he was taken seriously ill and partly paralysed leaving him bedridden an needing a lot of lookin after. I was one of the few people in the house that could understand him. His speech was slurred and difficult to understand it was like a strange language.

The old Marquis got used to me taking his meals and helping him feed...not that he ate much...and after a while insisted that I was the only one to look after him, he said the other girls had no patience and didn't understand him.

I didn't like it at first; his eyes seemed to look straight through my clothes, it made me uncomfortable until I learned how to deal with him.

In the hot weather when I wore a light bodice he would ask me to adjust his pillows time and again just to be near to me. I told him not to get too exited, as it was not good for him in his state of health; he just mumbled through his fallen mouth.'

At this point Nora gave Tom an embarrassed glance when the old lady looked into the distance to recall her time nursing the old man before continuing.

'On Sundays I walked down to the big house from here...my parents were his tenants...up and down that hill just to give him his dinner.

In between all that I was doing some of the maid's work and coming home to help my parents on the farm, my two older brothers had gone to America and part for a couple of scrawled letters, not heard from them since.

Almost every afternoon I had long conversations with the old man; it helped him sleep so he said. If another of the maids took my place he would refuse to eat and growl at them until they ran out of the room weeping.

Time and again the old Mr Boyle would ask me about my life at home, my friends in the town and the occasional ceilidh I went to in the evening, he said I made him think of his youth and looked forward to talking to me during his mealtime.

Sometimes he pointed to the big bible on the dresser for me to show him, my readin was a bit slow so I just showed him the pictures most of the time.

As the months went by I could see his health was getting worse, it got harder to communicate with him but I managed to understand his grunts and signs he made with his good hand.

Occasionally during family meetings young Mr Boyle asked me to sit in to help them understand what he was trying to say. They trusted me, they were my employers and they knew I would be discreet.

Sadly the old Marquis's condition gradually got worse, the poor man contracted a fever and being so weak wasn't able to fight it. Despite having the best doctor in the area in attendance, he died in his sleep the next day.

A month later I was summoned to the library. The new Marquis was there with an important looking man who I think was a lawyer as the desk was covered with rolled up paper tied with red ribbon.'

In a voice that made me wonder what I had done, young Mr Boyle said,

'I have something to tell you Miss Keene, first I would like to thank you for looking after my father. You made his last years a little happier and more comfortable so much that he indicated to us at our last family meeting that he wanted to amend his will to include you. You might wonder how we managed to understand him without your assistance; it wasn't easy we used one of your tricks that you taught him by helping him point to letters of the alphabet written on a board. It took a long time, we almost gave up but he insisted. You must have made a good impression on him Miss Keene.

We have read the will and I can tell you that in gratitude for your kindness and understanding he has left the farm at Carrowbeg including the ten acres to you.'

Then the other man turned to me and said, 'Miss Keene you would do well to keep the news of your good fortune within your family, not many are lucky enough to own the land they live on, you know how folks might twist it for their own ends.

This will be your land legally, no one will be able to lay claim to any part of it or remove you from it. I will draw up the documents…Deeds etc…in your name to own the farm outright now that you've turned twenty-one. It will be done within the next couple of weeks.'

'I can hardly remember what I said to them, my head was buzzing trying to take it all in and what it meant for my family. I would soon own a house land.

I think I thanked them at least three times before bowing and taking my leave.

Well Tom you can imagine my surprise, I flew up that hill eager to get home to tell my parents the good news.

Now you know how I came to own this farm; it is why I have been able to live here after Mr Murphy passed on.

What I've just told you is in confidence Thomas; it has kept many a one guessing how a widow can keep a place like this going. If you and Nora are serious and I hope you are, you will be taking on not just a wife but this farm as well.'

Tom glanced at Nora who was looking lovingly in Tom's direction, 'We are serious aren't we Tommy.'

'Yes we are,' Tom said weekly his face blushing almost the same colour as Nora's hair.

'Discuss what I have told you with your father Thomas. Remember to tell him that it's to be kept within the family and not to be repeated at least until you announce your intentions. I know I shouldn't but I'll leave you now to talk it over with Nora, I have work to do outside,' the old lady said easing herself out of the armchair.

Chapter 29

The Meeting…Tom joins the League

The League being a secret organisation, meant that until Tom was accepted as a member, the identity of the other members must be kept from him. Because of this, he was told to arrive after all the other members had assembled in the meeting room, which turned out to be the front parlour of the priest's house.

On their way into town Mick could see that his brother was quiet and apprehensive at the thought of meeting the members, 'You'll see some familiar faces, you'll be fine' he said reassuringly.

'Come on in,' Mrs Green the priest's housekeeper greeted Tom and his brother with a smile and what Tom thought was a wink…or perhaps it was a tick…when he arrived at the Priest's house.

'I've been told to show Thomas to the kitchen,' she said leaving Mick to make his way to the parlour. As the solitary candle she was carrying was the only means of illumination, Tom kept close to Mrs Green following her into the kitchen, where she
set about reviving the fire by adding more turf to the glowing embers at the bottom of the grate.
'Sorry it's so cold in here it's a big house to keep warm, would you like a hot drink,' the housekeeper said pointing to the large earthenware teapot keeping warm on the hob. Thinking he would be called into the meeting room before the old lady had time to prepare it Tom replied politely, 'no thanks, it's very kind of you Mrs Green.'

As it turned out there was time, time which was spent in conversation with the old lady. When Tom asked her whether she liked working for Father Quinn, she related the sad story of how she got the enviable position of housekeeper to the parish priest.

'He's a good man yer know, Father Quinn, not like some of the other priests ya hear about, he likes to talk things over if ya stray from the church's teaching, not give cruel punishments like some do. Yes he's a good man, he helped me.'

Two years previously on a late September evening, Mrs Green and her husband Shamus had been harvesting the last of their potato crop. After a long tiring day in the field they were filling the last sack when Shamus straightened his aching back, clasped his chest, and with an almost silent gasp fell face-down into the soil that he'd worked for the last fifty years and died instantly.

By coincidence a month before Father Quinn officiated at the Shamus Green's funeral, his aged housekeeper had passed on after falling down the church steps and suffered cracked a hip; later contracting pneumonia from which she never recovered.

At Shamus's wake the kindly priest took the now widowed Mrs Green to one side and offered her the post of housekeeper to be taken up when she felt she was able.

By now seven of the Ballingar Land League's committee members had assembled in the entrance hall waiting to enter the front parlour which had been set up as meeting room. Comfortable plush-leather chairs had been removed to another room, allowing the dark oak dining table to be extended to its full length with three matching ladder-back chairs on each side. An old hall chair embellished with the crest of some long forgotten landed family… made comfortable with two thick tapestry embroidered cushions…at the head of the table and two pine kitchen chairs at the other. A single oil lamp with a pale green bowl and fluted glass funnel sighted near to the heavily curtained window lit the room, casting shadows onto the half panelled walls causing a large Sacred Heart picture to appear to move within it's frame.

Father Quinn (the committee chairman) greeted each of the committee members with a blessing and a tot of poteen as they entered the room.

When all the members were seated and warmed with the fiery spirit, the priest brought the assembled Leaguers to order by tapping the table with an old ivory gavel normally used for church meetings. After an opening prayer and the preliminaries of thanking members for supporting the cause and taking the time to attend, he declared the meeting of the Ballingar Land League Committee open.

'Now dear friends I will start by reading the minutes of the previous meeting before turning to the nights agenda,' the priest announced .

That completed he glanced towards Mick and said,

'First item on the agenda tonight, new members. All new members have to be approved unanimously, that is by all branch members present', added the priest in case there was any doubt about the meaning of the word.

As expected Mick Walsh's motion to make his brother Tom a member of the Land League was passed and seconded without objection.

'Allow Thomas Walsh to enter,' the Priest announced.

Walking tentatively into the room Tom blinked to adjust his eyes to the brighter light. Looking around for reassurance he recognised the familiar faces of Dan Collins, Mick Fox, John Mulloy, Tim Cassidy, Jim & Ned Duffy and his brother Mick Walsh.

Tom stood at the head of the table to take the oath of allegiance repeating the words after Father Quinn whom then signed a specially printed Land League certificate, formally handing it to Tom with a warning that it could save his life, or cost him his life, be very careful and keep it safely hidden. Handing Tom a tot of 'the hard stuff' Father Quinn welcomed Tom into the branch, while the assembled members watched Tom down the poteen in one, causing him to cough and smile through watery eyes. The priest then shook Tom's hand and invited the new recruit to shake hands with each member in turn.

'Thomas please take your place next to your brother the priest gestured towards the empty chair next to Michael.

Mick gave his younger brother a reassuring wink and a pat on the back as he took his place at the table then whispered through the side of his mouth,

'That's Mick Fox's poteen, rough as hell.'

'Now to continue with the agenda,' the priest continued tapping the table.

'I suppose you've all heard the news that anyone that refuses to sell or give a service is to be charged with criminal conspiracy, this means we have to be careful how we make the policy work. The landowners refuse to halt the evictions despite pleas from Davitt and the big man himself Mr Parnell. Not satisfied with making our good people homeless, they're moving their own supporters onto the best land after the eviction. Giving them the land, 'land grabbers' the lot of em. We have to make a stand, tenants cannot be expected to pay ever increasing rents.'

The priest's sermon-like address stopped suddenly when Mrs Green's head appeared peering around the door, her hand gripping it as if her life depended on it.

Chapter 30

Samuel Daley is introduced at the meeting

'Yes Mrs Green,' the priest said a little impatiently.'

'There's a man here Father, says you will want to see him, I don't like the look of him,' she whispered.

'Ah thank you Mrs Green, don't worry I am expecting him, ask him to wait in the hall, I need to speak to the men first,' Father Quinn reassured her.

'Well dear friends, just arrived at our door is someone I would like you to meet, he's the son of an old friend I met when I was on mission in England.

He's from a good Clare family that were cleared off their land not long after surviving the famine. They settled in England near Manchester where his parents found employment in a cotton mill

Two years ago he joined the English army as an easy way of coming back to the land of his birth and was given the address of my parish by his father with instructions to contact me.

You all know we Irish have long memories and this young man is no exception and is looking for retribution for what his family suffered before and after the eviction. He is now working for us, passing on useful information about the movements of the army and the militia, this is how we know about evictions well before they happen, that's why we were able to help one of our members a few weeks ago.'

John Mulloy nodded his head approvingly as the priest continued.

'Only two other people in this room knew about this man, all will become clear later. If you will excuse me I will invite him to join us to be introduced to you all.'

Apart from Dan Collins and Mick Fox the members seated around the table looked mystified by what they had just heard.

Addressing the meeting Father Quinn announced in his most commanding voice.

'Gentlemen I would like you all to welcome Mr Samuel Daley, Sam to his friends.'

All heads turned to focus their eyes on the door. Out of the gloom a well-built young man emerged whom by the low light looked older than his twenty-five years.

Tom gave a barely audible gasp as he thought he recognised the young man. Each member stood and thanked Sam for coming back to his homeland. Risking his life by joining them to provide information about evictions. Tom waited his turn to enquire where he'd seen the man before while the valued young informant went around the table shaking each hand in turn.

Tom turned to his brother tugging lightly at his sleeve,

'I've seen him before, I just can't remember where.'

Before Mick could to respond Tom felt a hand on his shoulder.

'Hello you don't remember me do you? I was one of the men who stopped you on the road to search your cart then later it was me that called the two soldiers away to the Quay when the other two stopped you and your friend. Sorry if I was a bit rough, I had to make it convincing we have too much to loose.' Sam apologised.

Although Tom knew the tall young man holding out his hand was a friend of 'the cause', he found it difficult to respond as expected, he tentatively shook his hand and said, 'Right I'll remember that next time.'

'Now gentlemen we will continue with the agenda,' Father Quinn announced anxious to continue the meeting.

'First we need to consider setting up a fund to help those who are forced to turn to money lenders such as the Gombeen. For some borrowing money is necessary just to survive, it's a way of life, a constant battle. Many of my parishioners have large families to feed, with the landlords racking up their rent many are living on the edge. It's little wonder our people are forced to borrow money or are forced to leave our shores. There are almost as many of our fellow countrymen in America as here in Ireland, that's why Mr Davitt is in Boston raising funds for our cause, funds that can be used to help stop the evictions.'

'I agree, but who will manage the fund?' Dan Collins interrupted.

'We will elect a sub committee at our next meeting to look after and distribute any funds where it's most deserved. I will head the new committee and give advice based on information I have gathered around the parish.

Now gentlemen it's getting late I think we should meet again next Wednesday after the market. Think about what I said about setting up a fund and come back with any ideas for raising money.

Now as it's getting late for those who have to travel, I declare the meeting closed,' the priest announced with a final tap if the gavel.

Note: *Michael Davitt was an Irish republican and agrarian campaigner who founded the Irish National Land League. He was also a labour leader, Home Rule politician and Member of Parliament. Wikipedia*

Chapter 31

Martin's Lodgings in Birkenhead

Why do they build houses so close to one another? Land must be scarce in England, Martin thought looking at the terraced houses in the narrow streets running off the wider road carrying traffic to and from the docks. Narrow streets of houses all joined together, streets with children sitting on doorsteps chatting or standing facing each other playing 'pit-a-pat' games slapping their hands against their friend's whilst chanting a poem. Some of the young girls playing in the road were jumping over a piece of rope being held by two other young girls. Groups of raggedy clad boys playing games throwing pebbles at a wall or up in the air and catching them on the back of their hand.

This is so different to back home where we played in fields or more likely we'd be working in the fields planting potatoes or flax or on the farm feeding the livestock, Martin thought passing street after street that looked almost identical, checking their names with the one on the priest's note-paper.

Soon he was walking along one of the narrow terraces looking for a house with a number that matched the one the paper. At first he thought the house didn't exist until a man with a dusty black face delivering sacks of coal from the back of an equally dusty black cart, told him that the numbers were odd on one side and even on the other.

'F-F-Father Doyle gave me your address he told me to come here, he said you take lodgers,' Martin stuttered nervously to the man filling the small doorway of No 35 Filbert Street. To his relief the big man smiled and gestured him to enter as if he was expected, 'Yes young man we do, if the Father sent you you'd better come in.'

'I'm Jim Grogan and this is my wife Mary, that's our daughter Polly,' pointing to a little girl playing with a rag doll on a small rug in front of the hearth.

'Polly's three and we're expecting another before the end of the year,' he continued smiling at Mary who returned a coy smile.

'I'll show you your room, you can have the back bedroom, you'll have it to yourself as we have no other lodgers, I told Father Doyle we intend to have just the one.' The next morning at breakfast Jim Grogan started the conversation, 'Well Martin, mass is at eleven o clock you can come with me that is if you intend going.'

Martin scraped up the last of the porridge and said, 'Yes Mr Grogan I promised Father Doyle I would attend mass as I do back home.'

'Aye lad me names Jim, save Mr for the bosses.

You'll see some of the lads from the works at church I'll introduce you to them. Some are from over the water where we're from, well my father was, he's from Dublin, worked on the sailing ships then the steamers married me ma here and stayed.'

'Come on you two, you can talk later get yourselves ready you'll be late for church, Charlie will be knockin soon,' Mary chided struggling to dress a restless Polly in her best Sunday dress.

'That's Charlie and Sarah Jane next door we always walk to church with them and their two little uns,' Jim explained.

Chapter 32

Tom introduces Nora to his parents.

'Our Mick tells me you've joined the League,' Tom heard as he prepared to feed the chickens.

Turning he saw his father, one hand on his aching hip the other holding a basket ready to collect the morning's eggs, a chore usually done by Maria.

'Yes da I've something else to tell you and mammy,' Tom answered throwing the sack of corn over his shoulder. 'In the house when we've finished here, ya ma's got a pot brewing,' Joe said with a groan as he bent to lift the door on one of the nest boxes.

Seated beside the low arched fireplace warming her bones by the heat of the glowing turf, Tom's mother asked. 'What have you got to tell us darlin,'

'He's joined the league,' Joe said answering for Tom as if he wasn't there.

'Yes I've joined the league, I was going to tell you about that, there's something else to discuss as well as the league.'

Tom went on to tell his parents about his intention to marry Nora Murphy and her inheriting her aunt's farm and land at Carrowbeg. As soon as Tom mentioned the farm an land his father Joe ever the business man took more interest in the proposition saying, 'it looks like you've made a good match Thomas, when can we meet the young lady?'

'Please, this must be in confidence until it's all settled,' Tom said knowing they would comply.

'Of course we will, are you going to tell Mick and Maria?' His mother said looking at Joe.

'Yes, I think we can trust them keep it in the family until we make an announcement.' Tom said with confidence.

'That's what's been wrong with you,' his mother said with a smile. 'I thought you might be missing your friend Martin, when all the time it was about a girl. Walking about in a dream, I should have known.'

Changing the subject and thinking of his family's future Joe said. 'A farm and land Tom, sounds good, it might be a chance to expand the business.'

'Now, what's this about you joining the League Thomas?' his mother asked In her most serious voice. His father gave him a knowing look as if peering over invisible spectacles.

Tom went on to relate how he and Martin had witnessed an eviction on the way to Westport. 'How could I not join after seeing that ma,' he pleaded.

'We can't stop you son. Joe sighed wearily. I've told Mick to keep an eye on you and keep you out of trouble, if that is possible in an organisation that is pledged to make trouble,'

'We're pledged to stop the injustice, you saw for yourself during the famine years our people starving while food was sent abroad,' Tom answered with passion in his voice, quoting what he'd been told time and again whilst growing up among friends and neighbours that had lost loved ones starved to death when at the time food was being exported to England.

'Tommy we just want you to be safe and out of trouble, you can't help if you're locked up or worse, besides you have plans to settle with the girl Nora,' his mother said softly.

'Your mother's right Tom you must be clever when fighting for justice, use your head not your heart,' Joe said sagely.

'Now Tommy when are you going to bring your young lady here to meet us, you know we'll make her welcome. I'm sure Maria will be excited at the prospect of a wedding and a new sister–in- law,' his mother teased.

'On my next run to Westport I'll ask her to come back with me, she's a shy girl until she gets to know people,' Tom blushed.

The Wash holding was bigger than Nora imagined. It had all the appearance of a well organised farm, a large barn, pigsty and fenced off chicken runs.

The house too was bigger than she imagined, big enough for the large family it once accommodated. Soon, Tom would be leaving she mused as she entered into the homely warmth of the cottage.

'Welcome to our home Nora, Tom's been telling me all about you, his da will be here in a minute for his afternoon rest. He'll be pleased to see you after all the good things we've heard.' Tom's mother greeted Nora making room for her on the bench next to the fire.

The visit went well for Nora. Tom's sister Maria took to her immediately. His mother Mary smiled to herself as the girls chatted away. 'They would almost pass for sisters,' she said to Joe.

After what Tom thought was a successful introduction to his family it was agreed to set up a meeting with Nora's aunt to discuss their future. Before the young couple left for the journey back to Carrowbeg Joe declared. 'The joining of the two families can only be good for all concerned.'

Chapter 33

Martin at St Werburgh's

Martin found walking to church with Jim and his family a little different from walking to church back home in Ballingar. People still chatted about their family, the latest gossip and the weather. It's just like back home except for the better roads, more houses, bigger buildings in the town square taking all the light not much greenery. I'm sure I'll get used to it, Martin thought trying to remember the route for future reference even though he'd walked there the day before. At every adjoining street more worshippers joined the procession, greeting and seeking out friends as they walked. When Martin and the Grogan family arrived at St Werburgh's church the queue waiting to enter was at least fifty yards long giving Jim Grogan time to point out fellow workers from the yard.

Martin sat alongside the aisle giving him a good view of the congregation. The Grogan family and their next door neighbours Charlie and Sarah filling the rest of the row. During the service...which was almost identical to the service conducted by Father Quinn at Ballingar church...Martin was more interested in observing the congregation than paying attention to the service led by Father Doyle.

When Martin looked at the worshippers on the other side of the aisle he noticed something he never expected to see. All of the more recently migrated and mainly poorer families were sitting on his side of the church and the more affluent families were sitting on the other. With a few exceptions their were marked differences in the way they dressed. On the other side of the aisle the men wore better-tailored suits and the women wore more expensive looking clothes like the young girl he noticed sitting directly opposite to him. A pretty girl wearing a dark blue coat and a pale blue bonnet with a white lace frill and a silk ribbon tied in a bow under her chin.

Is she looking at me, or is she looking passed me? Martin thought, then he saw her smile, a feint smile more with he eyes than mouth.

Martin returned the smile using his eyes to avoid being noticed.

Throughout the service the pair exchanged glances a little more obvious each time and it didn't go unnoticed by Jim Grogan.

At the end of the service Martin followed the Grogan family out of the church, watched Jim place his weekly contribution in the large offertory box and realised he had no money to offer. Father Doyle seeing the worried look on Martins face said quietly, 'don't worry my son next week you will be able to make a contribution.'

'Thank you father,' was all Martin could think of saying with a long queue behind him waiting to exit the church.

Outside the church the worshippers gathered to chat and socialise, and again the groups were divided with the less affluent in a group to the left and the affluent to the right.

Jim introduced Martin to his friends from the Ironworks while his wife Mary chatted to friends and daughter Polly nursed her rag doll whilst watching a neighbours son of the same age kneeling on the ground playing with home-made toy ship on wheels modelled in the form of a paddle steamer.

Martin politely shook hands with the men from the yard, trying to look interested as he was introduced to each one in turn until his eye lighted on the young lady in the blue bonnet standing next to her parents. She was looking directly at Martin, her head slightly bowed her blue eyes looking his way through long lashes shaded by her blue bonnet.

Martin realised the exchange of looks with the girl didn't go unnoticed by Jim ; who gave Martin a knowing glance causing him to flush with embarrassment.

On the way home to Filbert Street Jim took Martin aside to warn him about the girl in the blue bonnet.

'Be careful Martin, that girl givin you 'the eye', she's a pretty face from a family with money, I know her da, he runs the pub at the corner of our street and wont like her mixing with anyone on our side that's why we sit apart. We are all of the same faith but we know our place, that's how we get along together.'

'Thanks for the advice Mr Grogan I'll remember that,' Martin replied thinking to himself, I'll be on the other side of the church one day.

'Jim, remember to call me Jim, anyhow there's plenty of good looking girls on our side Martin you'll see.'

Chapter 34

Tom is asked to keep watch

Passing through Ballingar on his way home after a long day collecting eggs, ever hungry Tom was thinking what his mother might have ready for his dinner until he saw Father Quinn standing in the church doorway as if waiting for someone. On seeing Tom the priest raised his hand for him to stop.

What does the Father want? Perhaps some eggs or something to do with the Land League, Tom guessed stopping the cart.

'Tom you collect eggs from a place near Knockmore don't you?' the priest said in a low voice.

Tom would have stopped to speak out of respect, now he wondered why the priest had an interest in Knockmore.

'Can you make it one of your last calls, I mean I would like you to pass through the place after dark. Take someone with you and let me know if you see anything unusual near the church.' Father Quinn continued again in a low voice.

'I'll ask our Mick, he'll want to come when I tell him you asked. What do you want us to look out for Father?' Tom asked looking puzzled.

'It's serious, it's also a church matter and it needs two people to look out for and witness anything unusual, do what I ask. On your way you'll pass Knockmore House I want you to note anyone helping to keep it functioning, you know, maids, gardeners, grooms and the like so that I can have a quiet word with them before our League members think about paying them a visit, there's been enough suffering best to avoid more. Report to me anything unusual you see when you pass the church, that's all I can say on that subject for now.'

The village of Knockmore was quiet the next evening when Tom and Mick passed through on their way home from collecting eggs.

'Why did Father Quinn want me to come with you Tom you always do this run alone?' Mick asked. 'All I know is that he insisted I have someone with me when to look out for anyone working for the 'big house' and anything unusual near the church,' Tom replied.

'Our boys are doing that already, there must be another reason, the only unusual thing we've seen today was that covered cart coming into the village earlier.

I didn't recognise the two men, I think that was a Dublin accent I heard when they replied to your greeting.' Mick mumbled grumpily.

'There's the church, Father Quinn wants us to report to him anything unusual he said it's a church matter. I think the big house was just an excuse,' Tom implied.

'I need to rest for a few minutes, these rough roads give me backache find a quiet place Tom.'

'When we get to the church we'll turn into the lane opposite and rest behind those trees, well have a good view of the church from there, if anyone's up to anything like robbing the silver we should be able to see them,' Tom suggested.

Chapter 35

Tom sees a vision

Under the cover of the trees in the lane opposite the church was the perfect place to observe the church without being seen. After ten minutes of watching Mick decided to take a walk along the road to stretch his legs, leaving Tom to look after the cart.

'I don't know what we're supposed to look out for it's getting really dark now, I'll have a walk to the corner by the church.'

Tom waited patiently alone with his thoughts about seeing Nora the next day to make plans for their future. He was woken from his day dream by a flash of light, a light that was shining up at the sky then onto the trees then slowly it moved upwards again until it stopped on the church wall. Tom blinked and looked in wonder at such a bright light, brighter than anything he'd seen before, move about on the church wall until the blurred outline of figures emerged, slowly coming into focus.

'Angels around a cross, they're angels on the church wall,' Tom said aloud looking around for Mick.

'Angels on the church trying to get into the church, they've come down on the light.' Tom said again looking around for Mick. Before Tom could say any more the light went out and darkness returned.

'Mick did you see that bright light on the church wall, the light that changed into angels, angels on the church wall.' Tom said excitedly when his brother returned.

'I saw a light shining towards the church on my way back that's all. I was coming back to tell you about those two we saw earlier with that big cart, they're around the corner hidden in the bushes opposite the church. The cart has a cover like a tent with a light inside, they're up to something those two.' Mick said.

'Come on Mick I'm hungry it's time to go, we can tell Father Quinn what we've seen tomorrow. He said tell him if we see anything unusual,' Tom grumbled holding his stomach. 'Yes I'm hungry too but I just want to see what's going on with those two feckers on that cart, I'd like to know what their game is and who put them up to it, who they're working for.

'Look Mick there it is again, look, look Mick on the church wall,' Tom whispered excitedly giving his brother a nudge that almost knocked him off the cart.

'What the feck is that, angels on the church wall,' Mick said in disbelief.

'Wait a minute, I think I know what's going on,' Tom said louder than was safe.

'I heard about a machine a few days ago in Castlebar, a black box with a light inside that makes pictures on a white sheet like magic. They said the machine was in the back room of a bar, the one on Castle Street.'

'Shush not so loud, you could be right, they're playing tricks I bet they're working for the English with their secret machine.' Mick whispered almost as loud then continued. 'It's time we got back to ma's cooking, we can tell Father Quinn what we've seen tomorrow.'

'We can have a good look at the wall as we pass the church,' Tom said taking up the reins.

A couple of minutes later Tom and Mick were staring at a blank church wall along with four of the locals from the village, one a young girl on her knees preying, her eyes firmly fixed on the wall.

'What's going on,' Mick enquired pretending not to know about the hoax.

'It's a vision, a holy vision, angels on our church wall six of them, and Mary and Joseph. We are blessed, truly blessed it must be a sign,' the man said quietly without turning his head.

'Will we see it if we stay?' Tom asked nudging his brother.

'Yes we've seen it twice tonight, the girl over there saw it first and came to tell us, she's seen it before she says it stops after the third time, she thinks it must be something to do with the trinity,' the man said crossing himself.

'It's a sign all right, how long has this been going on? Mick asked.

'The girl and a friend saw it a few weeks ago and reported it to Father Fallon, it's his church. He told her if she sees it again to be sure to have witnesses.

When she saw it again she came for us didn't she,' the man said glancing at the other two.

'Now Thomas tell me exactly what you saw and not what you think you saw,' Father Quinn said the next day when Tom and Mick called at the church in Ballingar.

'We passed by the big house in both directions all was quiet not much going on only the priest Father Fallon, he was the only person that we saw passing through the iron gates.' Tom began.

'Yes yes I know about Father Fallon he visits the house to say mass for the family and some of the workers brought over from England. It's good that he goes there as he picks up vital pieces of information on his visits.

Now what else have you to report young man?'

After relating what he and Mick saw at Knockmore church, the priest asked Tom to draw the scene and the four wheel cart.

Mick watched as Tom, sat at the refectory table making his best effort at sketching the church wall with six angels around a cross in the form of an arch, then he carefully drew a covered cart with a bright light shining into the pitch black night.

Without being asked Mick commented,

'That's exactly what we saw Father, I couldn't have drawn it better myself.'

'Well well gentlemen this is something you must keep to yourselves, promise me you won't tell a soul, and Thomas you've done well on your first job for the League you've both done well,' the priest said placing a hand on Tom's shoulder.

'Did you know about this father? Is that why you asked us to go through Knockmore at night? ' Mick enquired.

Father Fallon persuaded the girl...the one who saw it first...to put her mark along with his signature on an affidavit for the Bishop to consider. The Bishop will send a sealed letter by special courier to Rome to ask the Holy Father to declare the vision a miracle. This is why we must keep what you have seen to ourselves, we might be able to use this knowledge to advance our cause. The Bishop wouldn't want everyone to know it's a hoax, the hoaxers may have done us a favour. We can use it to bring our people together. We can tell our people that it's a sign that the lord is on our side, we must work together to fight the cruel landlords, we must make them stop the evictions.'

'What about the two feckers and their cart they could do the same again somewhere else,' Tom blushed realising what he'd said.

'When we catch the hoaxers with their machine they'll be warned off, their machine destroyed and the two feckers will be sent back to Dublin with a warning never to set foot in Mayo again,' the Father answered with a smile.

Chapter 36

Martin is taken on at the Birkenhead Ironworks…they start to build ships.

Martin walked with mixed emotions alongside Jim Grogan and what seemed like hundreds of other workers through the big iron gates with the name 'Birkenhead Iron Works' emblazoned on a wrought iron arch over the top. He felt nervous and excited at the same time at the prospect of working alongside the men chatting to one-another while waiting for an officious looking timekeeper to check them in.

Jim quickly led Martin to a small lean-to wooden hut set against a large brick building that he assumed to be the main offices. At least I've met some of the men at church, Martin reassured himself watching Jim confidently knock on the door.

Obeying the call to enter the office, Martin saw a large important looking man wearing an ill-fitting black suit with a waistcoat straining to contain his corpulent midriff, sitting at an old ink stained desk.

'This is Martin Mr Parker Father Doyle gave him my address and now he's lodging with us,' Jim said holding his cap in his hands and nudging Martin to do the same.

From the description Jim had given him the night before Martin took Mr Parker to be the yard foreman noting his black bushy eyebrows contrasting with his grey walrus moustache and wisps of grey hair escaping from under his bowler hat.

'D'you know anything about engineering son,' Mr Parker said looking at them both as if expecting both to answer.

'He says he's helped the blacksmith back home in Ireland Mr Parker sir,' Jim said answering for a nervous Martin.

'Let him speak for himself I'm sure he's got a voice,' Parker growled causing Jim to nod in embarrassment.

'Y-yes I went there with my friend after school and watched the blacksmith making things and repairing gates and wheels and er er ploughs,' Martin said nervously.

'Well that settles it, we don't have ploughs here lad, you can work with our riveting gang. Your first job will be to heat the rivets and pass them to the man doing the riveting, it's noisy and hot but you'll soon get used to it, and learn to shout.

Jim will show you where to go it's not far from the engine shop,' Parker said looking at Jim adding, 'Work as part of a team or you wont last five minutes, do as they say and you'll fit in. There's three others starting this morning, I always like to show new starters around the yard on their first day to give them an idea of what we do here.'

During the tour of the yard Mr Parker related the history of the works, how they changed from an iron works into a shipyard saying proudly, 'We have the skills here, that's why the owners decided to become shipbuilders and repairers. As the port expands the demand for ship-repair on the river will increase, hence the name over the main gate, Birkenhead Iron Works'

Chapter 37

Jim's house after Martin's first day at the yard

'How was your first day working at the yard Martin?' Mary Grogan enquired when he followed Jim into the kitchen.

'Fine Mrs Grogan, I'm sure I'll get used to it, the noise and the men.'

'And the heat,' Jim interrupted picking up Polly and kissing her on the cheek leaving behind a black smudge which Polly immediately rubbed off giving her father a look which said –you always do that.

'There's warm water in the sink and more in the kettle on the hob for you both to freshen up before dinner,' Mary said lifting the lid on a large saucepan to stir the contents.

At the dinner table Mary Grogan served a meal of what Martin thought was Irish stew and was keen to show his appreciation by scraping the last of the meat off the bone at the bottom of his bowl.

'That was very nice Mrs Grogan we have stew like this back home in Ireland.'

'It's called 'Scouse' Martin, around here 'Lobscouse' it's just the job after a hard day's work, would you like some more? Mary said pointing to the pan keeping warm on the hob.

'Yes Please Mrs Grogan,' Martin said politely.

'Get used to it Martin we eat a lot of it, except Sundays,when we have a proper joint of lamb and the leftover goes in the pot to make scouse on Monday and sometimes Tuesday,' Jim said looking pleased with himself.

'Not every Sunday Jim, it depends on how much money you bring home from the yard whether we can afford it, otherwise it's a cheap cut of mutton,' Mary corrected.

After the meal Jim settled in front of the fire with his newspaper while Mary bathed Polly before settling her down for the night.

Martin retired to his room and changed into the only other set of clothes and lay on the bed to rest his aching back after his first day's work, going over the day in his mind. He was almost asleep, his mind far away thinking about home in Ireland when there was a tap-tap on the door and Mary entered.

'Sorry Martin didn't know you were asleep, I came to tell you Jim is going to the pub down the road and is asking whether you would like to go with him.' She said holding the door open.

'Sorry Mary I've no money until the end of the week,' Martin replied looking embarrassed.

'Jim said not to worry about money you can 'settle up' when you get paid, he said he's going in five minutes after seeing Polly to bed,' Mary said with a look that said she wouldn't take no for an answer.

'Yes I'd like go, we wont there too late will we I'm a bit tired after working all day in that heat,' Martin replied.

'You'll be fine Martin,' Mary answered with a flirty smile that made him blush bright red.

Chapter 38

The Baker's Arms

Fifteen minutes later Jim and Martin were walking down the street towards a red brick building with a swinging sign showing a man holding a loaf of bread within a heraldic shield.

'It's a bit too convenient this place Martin, not everyone has a pub at the end of their street,' Jim said holding the door for Martin to enter the Baker's Arms public house.

'Hello Jim what you doing here on a Monday, must be something special,' John the pub landlord greeted the pair smoothing his handlebar moustache.

'My usual and the same for my friend Martin here, he started at the yard today and is staying with us. We called for a quick jar or two to show him our local hostelry and our jolly host,' Jim joked putting money on the counter while John pulled a pint of best mild.

'A new starter at the yard; welcome to our house Martin there's not many in tonight, it gets busy later in the week,' John said pulling the second pint.

Seated on a bench near the half stained glass window with 'The Baker's Arms' reading in reverse Jim explained, 'I don't usually come here on a Monday...can't afford it to be honest, Friday night after work is when most of the lads from the yard come here. I thought we could have a drink to celebrate your first day at the yard and introduce you to John the landlord. John's been landlord here for the last ten years, took over from a miserable old so and so who thought he could say what he liked to the customers, insulting them. He ran the place down so much that the brewery threw him out. John came in and worked hard, cleaned the place up, built up the trade again. Now it's a happy pub, part of the community. Even though John and his family sit on the other side of the church they're one of us, that was his daughter Jane I saw you eyeing up.'

'It was her looking at me Jim honest I just smiled back,' Martin flushed.

'You might see her in here, John lets her come in to collect and wash the glasses sometimes,' Jim teased with a wide eyed smile.

'If John's family go to church isn't this place open on Sundays and you say he's a landlord, landlords where I come from live in big houses and throw people off their land?' Martin queried.

'This pub is is owned by the brewery...Higson's, John pays them a rent and is the tenant we call the man running the pub the landlord, he opens the doors on Sunday at midday after church.'

The conversation stopped before Martin could respond when a door marked private opened and a young girl entered the bar. It was Jane only this time dressed in her every day clothes. Oblivious to the few people in the room Jane proceeded to collect the glasses and an odd pewter mug owned by the drinkers for their personal use.

'Put your eyes back son,' Jim teased watching Martin's eyes following the young girl around the room collecting the glasses from a nearby tables.

To Martin's embarrassment Jim said in a loud voice,

'Hello Jane there's someone here I'd like you to meet.'

'JIM,' Martin whispered his cheeks blushing like a beetroot.

'Hello Mr Brogan and hello to your friend,' the girl said politely acknowledging Martin looking directly at him with her deep blue eyes.

'Jane this is my new boarder Martin.'

'Hello Martin nice to meet you,' Jane said confidently.

Martin responded trying to disguise his Irish brogue with a hesitant, 'nice to meet you too Jane.'

Before the conversation could progress landlord John, seeing his daughter taking her time at their table called to her.

'Jane, you're wanted in the kitchen,'

'Must go father doesn't like me talking to the customers.'

'She's taken a shine to you, tread carefully Martin.'

Jim's warning fell on deaf ears, Martin was preoccupied watching Jane walk towards the kitchen.

Chapter 39

Tom and Nora at the Murphy farm

During the time Tom spent with Nora at the Murphy's he set out to prove his suitability to run a small farm, calling there at every opportunity. His hard work repairing one of the smaller outbuildings to make it suitable for sorting and packing eggs created a good impression with Nora's aunt. Not only did he impress Mrs Murphy, who was glad to see a man working about the place, but also Nora his betrothed who looked on with longing at Tom working around the farm. While helping him with some of the more simpler tasks she thought to herself one day they could be living here on this farm together as man and wife and they should set a date to be wed.

The opportunity came when she took Tom a drink while he was on an old rickety ladder repairing the barn roof where the thatch was missing. Looking lovingly at Tom through her long eyelashes with her head slightly lowered she held his hand and said quietly.

'Do you think we should set a date for the wedding Tommy?'

Luckily Tom on the ground leaning against the ladder when Nora asked the question for it took him by surprise even though it was what he wanted to hear. He was just waiting for the right time to talk about it.

Tom looked at Nora smiling as wide as his face would allow he quickly grasped her other hand, gently pulled her closer, looked into her pale green eyes and said teasingly,

'The sooner the better my dearest Honor.'

Before Tom could continue Nora squeezed his hand as if to hurt him and said,

'I'm sorry I told you my real name is Honor...Mr Thomas Walsh.'

Tom pulled her closer and chuckled, 'You'll be Mrs Honor Walsh soon.'

'Now then you two, your not married yet,' Mrs Murphy teased waving her stick walking towards them across the yard with a bucket of corn to feed the chickens.

'We were just discussing about setting a date for the wedding,' Nora said her face colouring as they moved apart.

Her aunt dropped the bucket, rubbed her back as she straightened and said with a knowing smile, 'About time, I'm not getting any younger, you know what I said about taking over the farm once you're wed. My aching back is getting worse, don't think I could make it up that hill much longer.'

'Nora has met my family and they like her, they agree we should be wed. With your permission Mrs Murphy I'd like to set up an egg business here as well as run the farm for you,' Tom said squeezing Nora's hand tighter.

'Well that's settled then, we'd all better start making arrangements to meet with your parents to set a date for the wedding, then we can talk about making the farm over to Nora or by then Mrs Walsh. It will be a good match for you both with this place as my gift, I know you will make the most of it Thomas.

It's time to move that old wedding trunk to your room Nora,' her aunt said turning to continue her chores.

Chapter 40

The Families Meet

On the day Tom and Nora arranged a meeting between her aunt and Tom's parents at the Walsh holding, Tom stopped to collected Nora and her aunt on his way home from his twice-weekly trip to Westport Quay. Due to the bones-shaking state of the roads and the boreen leading to Knockaun and the Walsh holding, Tom made the cart more comfortable for Mrs Murphy by the addition of layers of sacking covered with old woollen blankets.

To create the best impression for the visit, the day before the meeting, Tom's mother had Tom and his brother Mick limewash the front of the house, clean the windows and tidy the yard. Joe Walsh lined up three large carts with Joe Walsh and sons on the tail-gate within easy sight of the house.

Satisfied that enough has been done to impress any visitor, Joe and his two sons relaxed for the night helped by a nip or two, 'Just to test the quality,' Joe said with a twinkle in his eye while Mary prepared the supper while the men discussed the prospects of expanding the business.

'Welcome to our home Mrs Murphy.' Joe Walsh greeted Nora's aunt as Tom helped her down from the cart.

Nora remembering her previous visit to the Walsh house picked up her skirts and ran to Tom's sister Maria who was standing in the doorway.

Once inside the house the party took their places at the old oak topped kitchen table that had been set for the occasion with Joe Walsh and Tom sat on one side, Bridie Murphy and Nora on the other. Tom's mother Mary sat by the fireplace waiting to serve refreshments.

'Welcome again to our house Mrs Murphy and to your niece Nora, we are pleased to talk about the joining of our two families but first please accept our hospitality,' Joe said indicating to Mary to serve the food.

After the 'small talk' and enjoying Mary's baking accompanied by a tot of the hard stuff for the men and tea for the ladies, the negotiations began.

Expanding his business with his youngest son as a partner alongside his eldest son Michael was foremost in Joe Walsh's mind. He could see the potential of a base at the Murphy farm for his egg business twelve miles away and much closer to the exporter at Westport.

The more Joe thought about the alliance, more he liked it.

Bridie Murphy just wanted to pass on her considerable asset of the farm and land to the safe hands of one of her own family...provided it was a good marriage. Bridie Murphy was the first to lay out the dowry of the farm, including the house, offices (outbuildings) and ten acres of land. It would be signed over to Thomas and Honor (Nora) after the wedding, with the proviso that the couple made it their home and that she (Bridie) could live out her days there.

Joe thanked Mrs Murphy for her generous dowry, stating she had brought considerable assets to the table. He then proceeded to outline the extent of his haulage and egg collecting operation extolling the merit of establishing a new base at her farm to cover more of the county, adding his intention to make Thomas an equal partner with Michael and himself.

Bridie agreed that it would be a good business arrangement provided there were safeguards in place for Nora that gave her half of Thomas's share.

Joe turned to Tom who nodded in agreement then with a wave of his hand indicated to Mary to serve more drinks to celebrate before saying, 'Now we must think about setting a date for the wedding to join our two family's.'

Chapter 41

Choosing the day

The wedding of Thomas Walsh and Honor Murphy was arranged for June, as close to the beginning of the month as possible as Norah's aunt told her May is considered most unlucky for weddings.

Marry in the month of May, you will surely rue the day

'There's no time to waste, I'll take you both to see the priest in Westport, we need four weeks for the church to read the banns,' Nora's aunt said looking at Tom and Nora in turn.

A meeting was arranged with the priest at his house in Westport where he delivered the news that he was fully booked because of of couples wanting to wed before emigrating and is unable to officiate at their wedding in June.

'It's a busy time of year with people getting wed before leaving for England,' the priest said regretfully. The earliest date for a full wedding service is the last Sunday in May after that the third week in July.

Tom realised he had to find a priest to marry them in June; he knew that Nora's superstitious aunt and his mother would not agree to a wedding in May.

'Father Byrne, I'll ask father Byrne,' Tom said to Nora sounding a little desperate adding, 'Castlebar it's half way between Westport and Ballingar, it will be good for both families.'

'Your in luck Thomas I have a cancellation at the beginning of June, Sunday 1st June, the first Sunday of the month. I would have tried to see you right, I've had good a report about you from Father Quinn...joining our cause and finding out about certain goings-on in Knockmore,' Father Byrne said shaking Tom's hand.

Sunday 1st June 1879 was to be the wedding day.

Marry when June roses blow, over land and sea you'll go.

With the date set and the priest booked, Nora's aunt took command, 'Now the work begins, the big day will come soon enough. Nora, don't forget to write a letter to your parents telling them about the wedding. It's not easy finding the funds for such a long journey, they'll need time save money to pay for the boat crossing if they want see their daughter wed.'

Nora turned to Tom, her eyes fixed on his and whispered.

'Don't forget the ring.'

'So much to remember, so much to do we'll have to make a list,' Tom said in his most serious voice, adding, 'you make a list with your aunt and I'll make one with my ma, then we can compare lists encase we have forgotten anyone.

Remembering how Tom was missing his best friend Nora replied, 'good idea, don't forget your friend in England, Martin, and music, a fiddler, you said the one at the Quay was good.'

Tom laughed, 'This is harder than I thought let's just run away,' his face flushed when he realised what he'd said.

5 weeks later

Bent over the fire stirring the stew she was preparing for dinner, Nora's aunt turned and said. 'This wedding's going to be a smaller affair than I thought; with your father coming alone there'll only be three from our side. I lost touch with my cousins long ago I think they're in England or have passed on.

I'll ask my friends from the town and those from the farm down the road, that will make another five or six.'

'I know auntie, we talked about that yesterday me ma has to stay in England and look after the rest of the family, at least me da will be there to walk me down the aisle.' Nora replied as she stitched a bonnet for her aunt, adding, 'Tom said as long as there's enough guests there to make a good day of it, it doesn't matter how many there are, we'll be married and living together.'

At the Walsh house Tom's mother was also counting the guests, quizzing Tom about Nora's relations likely to be coming to the wedding.

'Eight, only eight, well I suppose with Bridie's family all gone...is your friend Martin coming Thomas?'

'You know what it's like ma, it was the same for our Joe when he went to Manchester, it takes a while to get on your feet and save money, paying rent an all, I'm still waiting for a letter. I'll ask his da,' Tom shrugged.

It was settled the wedding day was set for the first of June 1879.

With the preparations under way Tom spent most of his spare time at the

Murphy farm repairing the barn, fixing fences, and just being near to his betrothed.

Soon they would be Mr and Mrs Thomas Walsh.

Nora's only worry was Tom had joined the Land League and all agitation that entailed.

Chapter 42

The meeting at the forge, a raid is planned.

With just three weeks before Tom's wedding to his beloved Nora, he attended an informal Land League meeting at the forge.
Blacksmith Dan Collins was the first to address the impromptu meeting.

'As you are all aware we need more weapons, the few rifles and pistols that we have are old and dangerous, more likely to kill the user than the enemy.
To be taken seriously, to further our cause we have to arm ourselves with reliable weapons, weapons as good as the English.

In the last few days we've had good information from a very reliable source about new rifles shipped to Castlebar from the magazine in Dublin castle.'

Mick Fox smiled and raised his arms as if he was holding a rifle while the assembled murmured approval.

Father Quinn quick to answer raised his hand and said in his quiet persuasive manner, 'I know I have said many times it is wrong to take a life but I agree we must be able to defend ourselves. Where are these weapons, in Castlebar Barracks?'
I have information, also from a reliable source about the gun-room at the big house at Knockmore being restocked with new rifles, perhaps we should try there as it will not be as well guarded as the barracks.'

This suggestion caused loud murmur of approval from the Leaguers.

'I don't think we need to vote, the gun-room will be easier to break into than the barracks, it looks like we all agree with the Father Quinn's suggestion that we pay Knockmore House a visit.' Dan Collins said tapping the anvil with the mushroomed head of a chisel.

It was agreed by all to raid the big house at Knockmore that night to snatch weapons and any other useful items they could carry.

Three men were chosen for the raid, Mick Walsh with his cart and best pony.

John Mulloy and Jim Duffy volunteered saying, 'We have a score to settle.'

But for his impending nuptials Tom would have been first choice to go

117

alongside his brother, fortunately for him the priest intervened when his name was suggested.

'Sam Daley (the League's undercover man in the army) has been contacted via a secret drop-box for information concerning militia movements, he says they're all occupied at the Quay checking for arms shipments so you should only have the staff of the house to deal with. Be very careful I've heard the men have guns hidden,' Dan Collins warned.

'Where shall we met?' Jim Duffy enquired looking around the room for suggestions.

'Don't meet at a house. Meet at a quiet location where you're not likely to be followed. There's small lake near the big house at Knockmore I think you should meet there an hour after midnight, that's when I go about my business as you all know,' Mick Fox answered looking pleased that he had contributed to the plan.

Dan Collins agreed with his striker and continued giving instructions. 'You know what you have to do, anything that you pickup, guns or other items don't take them home, if they suspect you they will search your house, take them to the old abbey.

The grave nearest to the abbey's main doorway has been moved there. The grave's capstone covers an old entrance to the crypt. Slide the capstone to one side and you will see a ladder and some torches, don't light them until you have closed to stone back over the grave. That's where we'll store the weapons and any other things ready for sharing.'

The priest could see by the look on Jim Duffy's face that something was wrong.

Calling him by his Irish name the priest growled.

'Don't you like the plan Shamus?'

'I think it's a good plan Father it's just that I don't like confined places, it makes me panic and feel ill,' Jim said unable to look the priest in the eye.

'You can be the lookout on the top while we are in the crypt, there's plenty of cover in the ruins,' Mick Walsh interrupted, adding, 'It's not as confined as you think, I was there yesterday hiding the torches I made. The crypt runs the length of the old abbey and there's another way out through a small hole in the back wall.'

'It's settled then you three will meet at the lake an hour after midnight, wear dark clothing, and cover your faces. Mick, be sure to have a good pony on that cart, and be careful,' Dan warned turning to the priest for approval adding, we'll meet here tomorrow night to discuss how it the operation went and our next move.'

Chapter 43

Moonlighters raid the 'Big House'

Mick Walsh arrived at the lake with his best cart and favourite and most reliable pony at exactly one o clock in the morning. Peering around into the moonless pitch black night looking looking for Jim Duffy and John Mulloy he saw a light flare up and then out then light up again. Realising it was someone lighting a pipe he jumped down, patted the pony to stay and crept slowly towards the source of the light. Within fifteen yards he heard a voice that he recognised, it was Jim Duffy puffing away at his clay pipe whilst chatting to John Mulloy.

'Ya daft feker ya should know better than to show a light, put it out and lets be on our way,' Mick whispered.

The three 'moonlighters' entered the grounds of the house by walking along the banks of the lake...the poacher's way in and out.

Looking up at the imposing shadow of the castellated mansion against the dark sky, Mick thought, *what have we taken on, it's not like visiting a farmer to warn him off for helping the landlord.*

Luckily the house was poorly guarded allowing the trio easy access to the back of the building. All seemed to be going well until just as John was about to force open a small sash window with an iron bar a dog started barking.

'Feckin dog we should have known,' Jim mumbled.

'I'll deal with it I've got chicken guts in my bag,' Mick whispered throwing the contents of the bag in the direction of the noise, which ceased immediately.

'I wondered what the strange smell was,' John joked continuing to force the window.

'Quiet, someone's coming masks on' Mick whispered pointing to his face.

Jim pointed to the door and whispered, 'look, get ready.'

Someone was opening the door; one by one they heard the sound of heavy bolts being drawn. A hand holding a candle emerged followed by a man's head peering into the gloom straining through narrowed eyes to see what disturbed the dog.

The head hardly had time to see anything before Mick reacted by knocking the candle out of his hand, put his hand firmly over his mouth and wrestled the man to the ground writhing and making muffled noises through Mick's hand.

Jim stopped any further struggle by placing his knee on the man's chest while John held his legs. 'Now Mr, if you want to see the sun rise in the morning be quiet and take us to the gun room. You know where the key is?' Jim asked holding a knife to the man's throat.

'No I don't honest sir I'm just a porter,' the man pleaded when Mick released the pressure on his mouth.

'You lying fecker I bet you all know how to get at the guns in case of an emergency,' Jim growled prodding the knife at the man's throat causing him wince.

'Look boys I'm one of you, I'm Irish my name's Patrick like our saint, I was brought here from Dublin they offered good money when I was on the streets starving. If I help you you'll have to knock me out and tie me up or take me with you,' the man pleaded almost in tears.

'Ya still work for the English feckers, your coming with us we'll deal with you later, we don't have time to mess about tying you up so where is the key,' Mick said giving Jim a sly nudge.

Five minutes later John Mulloy and Jim Duffy and the now totally conciliatory porter were at the cart loading the haul of guns, ammunition and three sacks of corn while Mick covered the scene with a loaded pistol and a shillelagh in the other.

'These guns are new I don't think they've been used, I can smell the oil on them, John whispered picking one up and sniffing it.

'They are new, all of them, they were delivered last week from Castlebar,' the porter answered placing the last of the six rifles onto the cart alongside the two boxes of ammunition and the three sacks of Indian corn.

'Come on it's time we were out of here,' John said nervously,

'You what's yer name, what do they call you?' turning to the porter now lying tied down on top of the hay covering the boxes.

'Patrick Liam Burke untie me these boxes are cutting me to pieces,' he replied.

'You can walk if you want, that'll give you something to moan about,' Mick snapped geeing up the pony at the same time.

'Wait he'll be more use to us here in the house than taking him with us and having to hide him, it's that or'…Jim said gesturing as if cutting his throat.

'He's right Mick, think how much information he could pass on.' John said.

'Sounds risky to me,' Mick interrupted.

'Simple, ya daft feckers, the Priest comes in for confessions every week it's me that tells him everything, I know what goes on. I told you I'm one of you I was forced to work out here in this wild feckin place ya call Mayo,' the porter pleaded.

'Right we'll leave you here remember Patrick Liam Burke you're a marked man,' Mick warned.

'Soon will be,' Jim said showing a fist.

'Go easy boys,' the porter pleaded.

Five minutes later with the porter roughed up and tied to an iron gate in the walled garden, the trio set of for the abbey.

'Moonlight that's all we need,' Mick exclaimed when the clouds parted allowing an almost full moon to light the road leading to the ruined Abbey.

'Dan and Foxy said they would wait for us to show a light if it's safe,' Jim whispered as he scanned the ruins for a sign.

'There's a light on the top of the wall, and it's white moving side to side slowly, that means all clear,' John said excitedly almost falling off the cart as he stood up for a better view.

It was Dan Collins, carrying a loaded shotgun in one hand and a lantern in the other greeted the three Land Leaguers when they entered the abbey grounds.

After taking stock of the night's haul he immediately took charge, directing the men to store the guns in an empty stone coffin under the floor of the crypt and the sacks of Indian corn in a dry niche high above the ground ready for distribution later.

With everything stored safety Dan declared, 'Good job boys, now let's get home to bed, oh I almost forgot here's a bottle for each you of Mick's best poteen, take a nip or two to give the appearance of a drinking session,' then he tapped his coat pocket and said, 'we've had a nip or two while waiting here.

Chapter 44

Martin's progress at Birkenhead Iron Works

Mr Parker the yard foreman could see that Martin Cassidy was a quick learner, a natural engineer and quickly adapted to the kind of work at the yard, gradually earning the respect of his fellow workers.

Within a few weeks Martin progressed from heating and throwing red hot rivets to working with other trades. First the platers cutting and bending plates, then a week later when a labourer from the engine shop went off sick Martin was asked to cover for him where he found the work in the engine shop technical and more to his liking, it was also a lot less noisy.

Mr Parker noted that the young Irishman had an aptitude for mechanical tasks and Martin soon found himself summoned to the foreman's hut.

'Sit down young man,' Parker said to a puzzled looking Martin as he continued.

'This company has to keep up with the demand for more ships and has plans to expand. The workload at the yard has increased and trade on the Mersey is growing fast. Liverpool is becoming a major port serving the Atlantic routes, which increases the need for ship building and ship repair. We started as an iron works making iron, then because of our position on the river we turned to repairing ships, now we are making complete ships. Our owners want us to expand further to make us less reliant on other companies by making make our own engines, steam engines. As you have seen we already repair them and fit bought in engines into our vessels. Soon we will be making our own engines; the first castings are due to arrive next week. I have been asked by the board of directors to put a team together, a team of good men capable of building and testing large steam engines to start work as soon as possible.

Our owners have advertised in the national and local newspapers all over the country for experienced engineers and we are starting night classes in mechanical engineering for the most promising young apprentices.'

Six weeks later Martin was put to work with Andrew Cameron (known as Jock to the men) a canny old engine fitter from a Glasgow shipyard recently moved to Liverpool with his daughter and son-in-law.

The young Irishman applied himself to the task with enthusiasm gradually acquiring the various skills needed to build and test a steam engine. By applying what he learned from the lecturers at night school and old Jock Cameron's guidance, foreman Parker came to recognise Martin as a great prospect and he was soon promoted to assist a team of the engineers fitting the engines into the ships.

Martin had learned a lot in the short time he had been working at the yard and was now regarded as a prospect for further promotion. During a lunch break Mr Parker took him one side put his hand on his shoulder and said, 'Martin you've done well, your next step will be to learn how to commission the engines when they go on sea trials in the newly built ships. You'll be working with our experienced engineers learning how to check the engines and all the mechanical equipment in seagoing conditions.'

Chapter 45

Tom is arrested

It was just after morning prayers at Ballingar church when a very agitated Mick Walsh burst through the vestry door followed by Sam Daley still wearing his uniform under a great coat.

'Father Father they've got Tom, they've got Tom.'

'Shush not so loud there might be someone still in church, better come to the house where we can talk without being overheard,' Father Quinn said placing his finger to his lips.

'Now boys what's going on to make you burst in on me like that?' the priest asked once they were in the house.

'Them feckers, the English, they've arrested Tom,' Mick said almost tripping over his words.

'On his way back from the Quay, half way up the hill he was, two of them stopped him and they weren't English Mick, they were Ulster men working with our lot from England, Sam explained.

'Why pick on Tom he's a regular on that route to the port?' The priest asked looking puzzled.

'It was the cart, it was the feckin cart I should have known, it's the same cart that we used on the raid. Tom's cart lost a tyre and he carried on home on the wood till the wheel almost collapsed, since then he's been using the cart we used on the raid' Mick replied.

'You're right Mick,' Sam replied then continued. 'Someone recognised the cart on the night of the raid; it's bigger than most around here, they measured the tracks by the lake, they said they're wider than most of the carts in the area. One of the grooms from the big house reported that he saw the cart on the road by the hall that night and gave a good description of it. I heard the Ulster lot talking about it in the mess hall.' .

'There are other carts like it why pick on ours.' Mick said looking up to the heavens.

'Not that many make wide tracks like yours Mick' Sam suggested.

'What can we do Father?' Mick pleaded. He could face the firing squad or the rope if they find him guilty and we know he wasn't on the raid. We have to do something me ma thinks he's stayed over night at Nora's, she'll blame me for him joining the league.'

Later the same day Father Quinn, travelled to see Father Byrne in Castlebar to plea for help in obtaining Tom's release from Castlebar Barracks. Reminding him of the activities of the Ballingar branch of the Land League and how two of the members exposed the hoaxers at Knockmore Church. One League member being Thomas Walsh now in held prisoner in Castlebar Barracks with the prospect of facing the firing squad.

'Yes I have your papers hidden in my desk describing the exactly what the Walsh brothers saw. Was the lad involved in the raid at Knockmore House?' Father Byrne said raising his voice and pointing to his desk.

'No he was not involved, he was home in bed at the time of the raid, they've arrested him because someone recognised the cart. It was the one used on the raid because his usual cart lost a wheel,' Father Quinn explained.

'We need some proof that he couldn't have been at the Big house on that night, something believable that I can take to the Captain to plea for his release,' Father Byrne said sounding slightly agitated.

'We do, and it's urgent, as you know the lads getting married soon, besides he's innocent, he wasn't involved,' Fr Quinn said.

'We need a good witness to convince the captain.' Father Byrne mumbled as if thinking aloud.

'I was going to say he was helping repair the church roof but that would be in the daytime and wouldn't account for the night of the raid,' Father Quinn said looking at the ceiling.

'Nora's Aunt Bridie Murphy. That's it Bride Murphy might help. She could vouch for Tom saying he spent the night at her place, you know the old tradition around these parts of spending a night with the bride to be before the wedding,' Father Byrne said, his voice getting louder and nodding as if pleased with the plan.

'I believe it still continues in some parts with our church turning a 'blind eye,' Father Quinn agreed.

Thirty minutes later the Father Byrne's silver-topped walking stick was tapping on Bride Murphy's door. Seeing two solemn faced priests on the doorstep, a worried looking Nora enquired, 'Hello Fathers' what is it? Is it about the wedding? Don't say you can't do it?'

'It's not about the wedding Nora we're here to see you and your aunt, it's not good news I'm afraid, can we come inside,' Father Byrne said softly.

After some time talking to Nora's aunt while she comforted her now weeping niece, Father Byrne an Father Quinn convinced them both that the best way to secure Tom's release was to say that he spent the night at their house with Nora his bride to be, as was the old custom.

Satisfied they could do no more the two priests departed the Murphy house leaving behind Bridie comforting Nora armed with the signed paper that stated.

To whom it may concern,
   On the night of the 6th of May 1879 the night in question, Thomas Walsh stayed the night without leaving at my house in accordance with the old tradition of spending a night in the same room as the bride to be before their wedding.
 Signed, Bridie Murphy, Carrowbeg Farm

Chapter 46

The Barracks

Within twenty minutes of leaving the Murphy's the priests arrived at the wooden guardhouse set in front of the arched entrance to Castlebar Barracks. When Father Quinn saw the two elaborately clad soldiers brandishing bayoneted rifles approaching the trap and signalling it to stop, he asked turned Father Byrne and asked nervously, ' are we safe here.'

'Don't worry Father, I know the Captain he owes me a favour, I'm in here almost every week trying to settle minor disputes before they become too troublesome for him. Captain Malone is a lapsed catholic and respects the church,' Father Byrne reassured him while greeting the guards with the sign of the cross prompting the guards to nod their heads and raise their guns at the same time.

'We are here to see the Captain on urgent business,' Father Byrne said in his loud sermon like voice while looking down at them from the trap.

Immediately the more senior looking soldier sent his companion to inform the Captain of the arrival of two priests seeking an urgent meeting.

'The Captain will see you, leave the trap by gate and follow me,' the soldier barked opening the heavily reinforced wooden gates.

It was Father Quinn's first visit to the Castlebar military barracks; looking around he noted what looked like new recruits being drilled on the parade ground and coming from an older looking building with a veranda facing the parade ground the sound of musicians practising. There's a lot of activity going on here, they mean business, he thought before they entered the imposing double doors of the main building.

'What brings you here today Father Byrne, let me guess, is it to do with a certain young man we are giving our most gracious hospitality?' The Captain enquired sarcastically sitting at his desk cleaning his fingernails with a silver penknife.

'Yes Captain, Father Quinn and I are here to put matters right and help you and your officers with your difficult task of keeping the peace in our county,' Father Byrne replied ignoring the sarcasm.

Father Quinn quickly nodded his head in agreement.

Gesturing towards a row of chairs lining the wall opposite his desk the Captain said 'Please be seated gentlemen, I've been expecting a visit regarding this matter it seems we have things to discuss.' Once the priests were seated on the chairs closest to the desk, the Captain place his penknife on a polished brass standish and said, 'my Sergeant tells me we've questioned the young man and had the same answer every time, he says he was in bed at the time of the crime in question and knows nothing about it.'

'He's telling the truth he was in bed at the time you say a crime was committed, in bed but not his own bed. I have a signed statement here, signed by a lady well known in the town of Westport whose niece is be wed to the young man in question.

This fine upstanding woman states that Thomas Walsh spent the night of the sixth of May eighteen seventy-nine at her house many miles from the alleged crime,' Father Byrne replied sounding more like a lawyer than a priest.

Father Quinn then added as a reference, 'Thomas Walsh is a parishioner of mine, I can vouch for him as an honest young man and a good son of the church who is well liked in the area. He goes about his peaceful business of collecting eggs for export to England. You may have had the pleasure of eating eggs collected by him Captain.'

The captain looked at Father Byrne then down at his fingernails saying nothing as if trying to decide whether to believe his plea for Tom's release.

Before he could respond Father Quinn stood up made the sign of the cross and chanted, 'May the lord help you make the right decision and do what is right for this innocent boy, a young boy that has done no harm to man nor beast.'

The Captain picked up the document and saw that it was signed by Mrs Bridie Murphy and witnessed by the two priests.

'Please sit down Father I don't need preaching to I gave up the church long ago but I will accept this signed paper as the truth as I said we have questioned the young man and he denies being anywhere near where the raid took place,' the captain said ringing a brass bell on his desk.

Almost immediately an aged looking soldier with a grey walrus moustache and bushy sideburns entered the room, clicked his heels, saluted and stood to attention facing the Captain.

Through narrow eyes as if trying to convey a message the Captain commanded.

'Bring the prisoner Thomas Walsh he is to be released, no restraints and return any possessions to him immediately'

Five minutes later Tom walked into the Captain's office followed by the walrus moustached soldier. On seeing the two priests...now standing ready to greet him..a hint of a smile appeared on Tom's bruised face. With Tom stood head slightly bowed facing the desk the Captain said looking at the priests for approval.'You're free to go young man, fortunately for you the Fathers have produced evidence that proves to me you could not have been involved in the raid we have no choice but to believe your story.'

A cheeky grin lit Father Byrne's face as he said, 'Thank you Captain, justice is done, can I expect to see you in my church on Sunday, we welcome everyone.'

Father Quinn instinctively made the sign of the cross again before the holy fathers escorted Tom out of the building chanting in unison, 'Bless you captain.'

Chapter 47

A night at the Murphy's

Once clear of the barracks, Tom, glad to be on his way with his own cart thanked the two priests for securing his release saying, 'the feckin soldiers wouldn't believe me. I told them I didn't know about any raid on the house and it would have been worse only for our man Sam Daley, he took over from the others trying to make me admit being on the raid.'

'You're safe now Thomas get yourself to the Murphy's, it's arranged for you to stay the night there and get cleaned up so you'll look better after the roughing up they gave you when your ma sees you tomorrow,' Father Byrne reassured.

'Thank you for all you've done Father I'm fine, you've both done enough.'

Looking pleased with the outcome Father Quinn said, 'I'll call at your place Tom on the way back to Ballingar to give your brother Michael the good news, it's not far out of my way.'

Despite sheltering under the branches of an overhanging tree at their meeting place by the marker stone to waiting for Tom to return from the Castlebar barracks, Nora was cold, wet and shivering from the storm that had just blown up. After waiting wrapped in her red plaid shawl for what seemed like an age she saw a cart coming into view and it was Tom holding the reins; the priests had secured his release. Holding her skirts above her ankles, her curled auburn hair escaping from beneath her green and red plaid shawl the young colleen ran to meet her lover. Nora raised her skirts further skilfully avoiding the pools of water, leaning against the driving rain that was trying to stop her progress,

Seeing Nora running towards him Tom waved then tried to urge the reluctant donkey to a faster pace. A few seconds later they were in each others arms, when Nora released Tom from her vice like embrace she asked, 'what have they done to you Tommy?' pointing to a bruise on his face

'It's nothing don't make a fuss, it's just well, it's just when I told those English what I thought of them for locking me when I was not involved in any robbery, they thought they'd teach me a lesson, thank goodness Father Byrne thought about the old ways and traditions before a wedding and gave the Captain the letter from your auntie, otherwise I'd still be there locked up. Now let's get out of this rain.'

Five minutes later Tom and Nora were sitting in front of a glowing turf fire drying each others hair with the rough blankets Nora's aunt used as towels. Pointing to Nora's bedroom on the mezzanine her aunt said in her most serious voice, 'Nora, get out of those wet clothes before you catch a chill, you can change in your room. Thomas, you can have my husband's old clothes, there should be something to fit you in the chest at the end of my bed, you can change there, bring your wet jacket and the rest for me to dry then we'll look at those bruises and that swollen lip.'

Nora had changed and was stirring a bowl of chicken broth when Tom came out of the bedroom feeling self-conscious wearing Mr Murphy's everyday clothes.

'My face is fine, it looks worse than it is,' Tom said not wanting a fuss his or anyone touching his swollen lip.

'You'll be fine for the wedding, now this should warm you both up, then we'll talk about the sleeping arrangements,' Nora's aunt said handing Tom a bowl of broth and trying to look stern at the same time, although Tom thought he detected a twinkle in her eye. 'I know the old custom of sleeping alongside the 'bride to be' before the wedding is still going on in some parts; it's not heard of much now around here and definitely not in my house. Nora, you will sleep in your own bed. Thomas, I have a spare straw mattress and blankets you can sleep here next to the hearth,' the old lady said in a voice not to be disobeyed.

Later that night when Nora looked down from the mezzanine she could see Tom was fast sleep blanketed in the warmth of the old stone fireplace. An hour later Nora was awakened by whimpering cries from below.

'Tommy Tommy what's is it Tommy,' she whispered soothingly,

'Tommy it's me Nora, shush Tommy it's me your Nora it's over you're safe you're here with me. Tommy it's it's me Nora, Tommy you was crying out, *stop it I wasn't there,'* Nora whispered gently rubbing his shoulder.

'Sorry I must have been dreaming I was back in that dirty cell they threw me in, they tied me to a chair and started roughing me up till our man that Daley fella took over, that's what it's about.' 'Try to get more sleep you'll feel better in the morning,' Nora said putting her arms around him and hugging him until he winced with the pain in his ribs then gently kissed his face and whispered softly, 'Sleep tight Tommy, soon we'll be married and spend every night together.'

Chapter 48

Martin's attraction

Living in a small house alongside the Grogan family, Martin, a likeable good looking young man was made welcome and treated as one of the family.

His occasional letters home, as well as sending what money he could spare, reassured his mother that he was in good health and being well looked after by Jim and Mary Grogan. In his first letter he knew they'd be pleased when he told them that he'd found a job with good prospects, working in a shipyard, not in the port of Liverpool but in a growing town on the south side of the Mersey called Birkenhead.

It was true he was being treated well by the Grogan's and was being teased at work by other young apprentices for being lucky to live in the same house as Jim's attractive wife Mary.

Martin had been aware from the first moment he saw Mary that she was a very elegant lady, pleasing on the eye and she knew it. Martin sensed danger, and in the desire to be accepted into their home as a lodger he put all carnal thoughts at the back of his mind, concentrating on studying his technical books in his room.

After a month living in close proximity to this good looking young mother he found himself more attracted to her every day. This was not helped by Mary's flirty nature, twisting her husband and Martin around her little finger, flirting with them get her own to way.

At times it was as if she had two husbands apart from the fact that only Jim shared her bed. Martin resisted any temptation by thinking about Jane the publican's pretty daughter and reminding himself that Mary is a married woman, 'out of bounds' and pregnant...her condition becoming more obvious every day.

Martin was now seeing more of Jane. Every morning when he passed the Baker's Arms public house on his way to work Jane would be near a window waiting to wave to him when he to passed by. On his...by now regular...Friday night visits with Jim to the 'Bakers Arms', every time Jane came to tidy their table she took her time, always smiling at Martin and with the hostelry being very busy on Fridays evenings they were able to indulge only briefly in small-talk.

By the fourth week Martin could see Jane might be willing to meet him somewhere where they could talk rather than a few polite words and smiling at each other in a crowded pub. When Martin discovered Monday was her night off as the trade was the slowest, he took the opportunity when Jane came to his table to collect the empty tankards to discreetly pass a note hidden under a glass suggesting that they meet in the town library at 7 pm on Monday evening.

Chapter 49

The Library

For Martin Monday evening couldn't come quick enough, Mary and Jim Grogan could see that he was consuming his dinner faster than usual and failing to use the bread crust to mop up the last of the tasty scouse gravy still covering the bottom of his plate.

Jim glanced at Mary giving her a look that said he's up to something. 'What's the hurry Martin you'll make yourself ill eating so fast,' Jim enquired with a wide eyed smile that said I think I know the answer.

'No hurry just going to the library, want borrow an engineering book before one of the other lads take it,' Martin blustered not looking Jim in the face.

'Leave the lad alone Jim he's got his studies as well as other things on his mind,' Mary teased holding her pregnant belly and trying to look serious at the same time.

There was a certain amount of truth in Martin's reply as he knew other students in his night class were also using the library to further their studies.

By five to seven Martin was sitting at a long oak table in the library with his night class notes on one side and a borrowed engineering text book on the other. His coat placed on a chair next to him reserving the place for Jane, not that anyone else was likely to sit there.

With every movement in the room Martin looked up from his notes hoping to see Jane walk in rather than another student looking for a quiet place to study.

Unable to concentrate, looking up at every sound in the building Martin glanced hopefully at the black cased wall-clock it's big hand pointed to the Roman numeral one, it was now five past seven, where is she? Perhaps her father has other plans for her. Ten minutes past seven, she's not coming, Martin listened to the slow monotonous tick of the clock, was it mocking him? He asked himself. The big hand was now on the three bars making the Roman numeral three, it was now fifteen minutes past seven, the clock was mocking him...tick tock tick tock she's not coming tick tock tick. Just as he was giving up hope of his first meeting alone with Jane and thinking he'd better make use of the time by getting on with his studies, one of the opaque glazed double doors opened and a red faced Jane walked in wearing a dark blue coat not unlike the one she wears to church. With a quick glance around the room she chose a book at random from the nearest shelf before carefully removing a light blue shawl from her head to let it drape loosely over her shoulders. Jane paused by the bookshelves holding the book as if it was what she wanted to study, giving her time to decide where to sit, choosing to sit at the table opposite Martin slightly to his right.

Before Jane had chance to speak Martin whispered, 'I kept a seat for you,' pointing to the chair next to him.

'Better stay here for now,' Jane replied in a barely audible whisper stretching her legs until their feet touched causing Martin to react with a loving smile, at the same time placing his hand on the table as if inviting her to do the same.

Martin realised the library gave them a chance to meet without causing too much fuss from her parents although it was not the best place to communicate. For the next hour the besotted couple, besides looking into each others eyes and discreetly touching hands, from time to time passed notes to each other using the back pages of his notebook. The last one from Martin asking to walk Jane home saying, it will give us time to talk besides you shouldn't walk home alone in the dark.

On the way home from the library, to Martin's surprise Jane did most of the talking questioning him about his life back in Ireland and other people in his life.

Martin still trying to adjust to life in a big bustling town like Birkenhead preferred not to talk about his family whom he was missing so mutch.

'I've had a letter from my best friend back home inviting me to his wedding in June,' Martin said.

'Will you be going? When is the wedding? What's his name? Who's he marrying?

'That's a lot of questions, now lets see. His name is Thomas Walsh he is the same age as me and he's marrying an English girl from Liverpool called Nora Murphy.

'The wedding Martin when is the wedding and are you going?'

'Don't know yet, it's the first day of June, it's the first Sunday in June and it depends on the boss at the yard. I mentioned it to Father Doyle yesterday after mass, he said he'd see what he could do. I'll ask my boss Mr Parker tomorrow morning after he's had his breakfast; he brings his breakfast to work that how he get to work early, he's always the first in. He eats his breakfast in his office when all his men are in through the big gates and working and before the top bosses come in.

Chapter 50

Mr Parker's Office

'Yes lad I've had a note from the Father, I think it can be arranged, I already planned to put you and another lad with the sea trials gang to gain experience of how we test the engines and other equipment at sea.' Mr Parker said the next morning when Martin stood in front of him with his oil stained cloth cap in hand.

'We usually send an apprentice or two to check the bearing temperatures on the engines, it's literally a hands on job feeling the bearings once they reach their running temperature. They stop the engine occasionally to check the moving bearings on the con-rod and the cross-head. He added picking his tea stained teeth with a tie pin to remove the bits of meat that refused to be consumed.

'What's the date of this important wedding?'

'It's June the first Mr Parker, I would have to be in Westport County Mayo by the thirty-first of May at the latest,' Martin replied nervously looking at a spreadsheet on the office wall that indicated the progress of the vessel in mind.

'You're lucky, we have a ship almost ready and it will need two weeks of sea trials starting around Monday twenty-sixth of May. I'll give you a note asking them to put you ashore in one of the lifeboats on the twenty-eighth , they have to test launch the lifeboats and like to do it near the shore. There's a flat beach north of Dublin at Malahide, I'll put that in the note asking the Chief to do the tests there. You've a week off work with my permission. Don't expect to be paid once you leave the ship and remember to take money as you'll have to make your own way back to Birkenhead. There's at least one steamer crossing to Liverpool every day, I want you back here by Thursday 6th of June, don't let me down. Now get back to work you've a lot to learn before then.'

Mr Parker said pointing to the door.

Chapter 51

The League Takes Stock

After the events of the last two weeks, Father Quinn decide it was time to hold a meeting to take stock of what the Ballingar Land League had achieved and what else can be done to further their cause. The meeting was called for six pm the following Monday night in the back room of Campbell's Bar. Wisely changing the venue to reduce the risk of being followed, Timing it early enough not to cause suspicion as to why the men were in the town, knowing they sometimes liked a drink before their evening meal. Also six pm was late enough for the the members to return home under the cover of darkness if they stayed behind for a drink after the meeting. Through his contacts at the Barracks Father Quinn had good information that Monday was when most of the Militia had a night off after the usually busy weekend, leaving only a small number of soldiers to cover the district.

Campbell's Bar was quiet when Tom and his brother Mick arrived. Tom noticed the Rooney brothers in their usual seats as they passed through to the back room.

Don't they ever go home? Are they afraid of someone taking their seats next to the fire even when it wasn't lit? Tom thought following Mick to the back room to see Father Quinn with his back to them sitting at the table studying his notes.

Tom and Mick were the first to of the ordinary members arrive. Paddy Campbell...the trusted owner of the bar...and the priest had set the room up for the meeting by moving Paddy's kitchen table against the back wall and setting chairs in a semicircle with the most comfortable upholstered chair reserved for the Priest. Mick put his coat over the back of a chair and indicated to Tom he was going to the bar for the drinks. Father Quinn occupied himself at the table writing the agenda for the meeting in a note book in which he kept his thoughts for his Sunday sermon.

Since doing repairs to the buildings at Nora's aunt's farm Tom saw things in a different light. Looking around the room while waiting for Mick to return, he observed the ceiling in the bar stained dark brown due to years of tobacco smoke and the walls with patches of plaster missing, revealing the wattle and daub construction beneath.

Gradually the semicircle of chairs became occupied. Each of the members holding a jar of ale apart from Father Quinn, Mick Fox and Dan Collins all of whom favoured a tot of the 'hard stuff', a better quality poteen that Paddy Campbell kept for favoured customers.

Standing straight backed to his full five foot six height, notes in one hand, looking over his spectacles balanced on the end of his nose Father Quinn tapped the table behind him with his empty glass and in his most authoritative voice above the murmuring of the assembled members brought the room to order.

'Gentlemen, gentlemen GENTLEMEN, we have things to discuss, I declare this meeting open.

I called this meeting to thank you all for your support and good work since we formed our Ballingar branch, fighting for justice, fighting the enemy all around us not only here in this corner of North Mayo but in all corners of rural Ireland.

As an organisation we are growing in numbers every week as more branches are formed cross the country. Now we must take stock and make some important decisions. Thanks to the generosity of our friends in 'The Big House' we now have enough weapons to defend ourselves or threaten those helping or working for the landlord.'

'Yes very generous,' Jim Duffy murmured.

'This means we also have the means to kill.

Killing is against all my teaching.

Killing is against all my instincts.

Taking a life must only to be used as a last option.'

The priest paused and turned his head to look directly at each of the leaguers in turn.

'The weapons are stored in a safe place and from what I've been told are of the latest type, some new recently shipped in from Dublin.

Our help and support given to the poor souls thrown off their land is a great comfort to them as some of you in this room will know. Unfortunately we cannot help everyone, but we can make life difficult for the absentee landlords and their agents. Until the law is changed to stop the persecution of our people by those who stole our land and now charge us for living on it we must continue the fight.

Now about Tom's arrest and imprisonment, with the help of Father Byrne and the co-operation of his future mother-in-law we were able to convince the Captain at Castlebar Barracks of his innocence to secure his release.'

Father Quinn paused when he noticed Mick Walsh's raised hand.

'Do you have a proposal Michael?'

Influenced by his mother's warning that should anything happen to both brothers, if they were captured or worse the Walsh family business would be in danger.

Mick Walsh proposed...to Tom's embarrassment...that he should be to be a special case due to him being the youngest member and his forthcoming nuptial.

After a short discussion it was decided unanimously that Tom should not be put at risk by taking part in any dangerous operations.

Father Quinn looked at Tom nodding his head as if answering for him and said.

'Thomas you can serve us by being our eye and ears of the district; your rounds cover my diocese and most of Father Byrne's. Yes Thomas, you've gathered useful information in the past.'

'Thank you Father I've always looked out for our people, seeing an eviction for myself makes me more determined to rid our country of what history tells us are invaders.' Tom said with surprising emotion.

Again the room buzzed with approving comments causing the Priest to raise his voice to regain order.

'Gentlemen, gentlemen, the hour is late we must bring this meeting to an end soon as we need time to disperse without raising suspicion. The next official meeting will be at the usual time and place.

To conclude gentlemen, you might have heard of strange happenings in a place not far from here, it's been fully investigated and a report has been prepared by Father Byrne and dispatched to Rome for consideration by the 'Holy Father'.

I've heard from the bishop that they're keen to keep the report quiet, he thinks it could be a way of uniting the people and as it's a very sensitive subject I ask all our members not to discuss it in public.

Thank you gentlemen and safe journey home.'

Chapter 52

The List

With only a few days left until she was to marry into the Walsh family, Nora thought it would be a good idea to arrange a meeting with Tom's sister Maria to get better acquainted, and to discuss the final preparations for the big day.

Three days earlier Nora had sent a note with Tom to arrange the meeting with Maria at her aunt's farm, suggesting that she could ride with her brother on one of his trips to Westport Quay.

When Tom and Maria arrived at the Murphy Farm, she teased her brother. 'You can go now, we girls have things to discuss.'

'I know when I'm not wanted, don't think I'm going without seeing Nora.' Tom replied pretending to sulk.

Before Maria could answer a smile as wide as the bay lit Tom's face when Nora appeared in the doorway.

'Tell him he's not needed Nora, we have women's work to do,' Maria teased on seeing her future sister in law.

Nora answered by running to Tom, pulling him down from the cart and embracing him as if he'd been away for a year even though it was only two days.

'Sunday will soon be here, don't want to be doin things last minute,' Mrs Murphy said to Nora, fussing as aunt's do

'That's why Maria's here, we're making a checklist auntie, look'.

'What's a checklist darlin?

'It's a list of all the things we have to do before the wedding.

'You're writing a list; waste of time with my old eyes.'

'I'll write it in big letters and put signs on like on the the shops, then we can look at the list together, see like this I'll draw a picture of a ring for the wedding ring and a cake for the wedding cake. We cross them out when they are done, Nora said looking pleased with the idea. Picking up her shawl from behind the door her aunt replied, 'It looks like a grand idea, I'll leave it to you girls for now, I've work to do outside, I'll look at your list later.'

Nora and Maria chatted as if they had known each other all their lives going through and adding the items to the list they thought was needed to make the wedding a success. The one thing that concerned them both was the involvement of Tom in the Land League. Maria had heard talk in Ballingar about women supporting their men by raising money. Sensing Nora's fear for Tom's safety she turned to Nora to try to reassure her.

'I know you're worried about Tom being in the League, him being locked up and them going out late at night fight the cause, the men feel they have to do something when they see our people being made homeless.'

'It's just that I think about him on the road collecting eggs. You know what it's like Maria, soldiers with guns and the road blocks I feel so helpless,' Nora worried.

'There might be something we can do. I've heard that the women in some towns are getting together to raise funds for their branch of the League. They feel they've got to do something rather than sit at home worrying what their men are up to. They can't join the men but they can help by raising money,' Maria said.

'If the women of Westport ever get together I'll be with them,' Nora replied enthusiastically.

Just then her aunt returned carrying a basket of eggs, easing herself into her favourite chair by the fire, she asked.

'How's the list coming along girls? Doesn't look much different, have you thought about decorating the barn? Is that on the list?'

'Yes auntie, Tommy said he would decorate the barn with help from a friend.

Don't know which friend with Martin gone away, Tom wrote to Martin three weeks ago inviting him to the wedding, not had a reply yet.'

Nora smiled at Maria and added, 'The priest, the fiddler, the cake, the guests all ticked off, and my father will need a bed making up, he said he's staying at least three nights. That's the list done, unless you can think of anything else auntie.'

Chapter 53

The Visitor

To Tom's surprise getting up early the day before he was due to wed the love of his life felt like any other until he was half way down the boreen on his way to Westport. His head began to spin with all the events of the last few months; it was like his life was passing before his eyes. His heart raced, his nerves played tricks thinking he must avoid the potholes in case he damaged the eggs even though he was only carrying rope and twine to finish decorating the Murphy's barn.

He thought of the day that he first saw Nora walking down the hill to the bakery carrying a wicker basket as she hadn't a care in the world. He smiled to himself when he thought of the time when he offered her a ride on the cart and refused, then how he felt when she coyly accepted when he offered again.

He thought of his friend Martin, their childhood together in Knockaun and the eventful journey after picking him up from his parents house to take him to Westport to catch the steamer to England.

Since taking his friend Martin to catch the steamer at Westport Quay on his regular deliveries of eggs to the exporter Tom would often see Martin's cousin Paddy and call at Matt Kelly's bar for a quick jar or two before picking up his cart from Ned O'Malley's yard. On his last visit to the quay Paddy offered to help Tom prepare the barn for the wedding celebrations.

Having arranged to have the morning off work at the docks, when Tom arrived at the boreen leading to the Murphy holding Paddy was sitting on the marker stone.

'I've brought some extra help,' Paddy said trying not to smile.

Thinking Paddy was about to play a trick. 'Where? We arranged for just the two of us Tom said suspiciously.

'Here's your extra help,' a voice behind him said. Recognising the voice Tom turned to see his friend Martin step from behind a nearby tree.

After the initial shock of seeing his best friend, Tom, keen to learn how Martin had been doing in England for the last few months.

'Tell me all about England, what is Liverpool like? Where are you stayin?' Tom questioned Martin on their way to the Murphy farm.

'I got your letter Tom, didn't answer straight away because I didn't think I would get the time off, with not long starting the job at the yard, till I mentioned it to our priest Father Doyle after Sunday mass. He's a very caring man, says he loves the old country and thinks we should keep in touch with it. The next day he sent a message to my boss Mr Parker, he owed a lot to the father and was never likely to refuse him anything.

Luckily one of our ships was completed and due to be tried out at sea, 'Sea trials' they call it, Mr Parker arranged for me to work with the engineer testing the engines.

We arrived off Dublin two days ago the crew put me shore at Malahide then I made me way here by hitching a ride to Westport to stay with Paddy for a few days.

Oh and by the way Tom, I'm not living in Liverpool, I'm the other side of the river in Birkenhead it's a town separate from Liverpool, you put Birkenhead Liverpool on your letter, your not the only one, me mar got it wrong as well, she says I'm working in Liverpool. I'll tell you all about my lodgings and the nice family I'm staying with later,' Martin said jumping down from the cart, as Tom stopped the cart at the barn.

'Lets get the job done lads, we can talk as we work,' Paddy interrupted remembering they had work to do.

The trio soon had the barn and the front of the house looking suitably festive. Freshly whitewashed and garlanded with newly picked flowers freshly gathered by Nora and Maria, even the large marker stone and all the stones of any significant size along the boreen were treated to a fresh coat of whitewash.

During the work the three friends listened eagerly to Martin telling of the events and his experiences since leaving his home in Mayo for a new life in England. Like the long voyage around the coast of Ireland to Liverpool on the steam packet. Being told by a policeman that his contact was a priest in Birkenhead on the opposite side of the river Mersey to Liverpool. How the priest helped him find lodgings with a good catholic family and a job at the Iron Works and the hardest thing for anyone emigrating from the beautiful green countryside of Mayo's Atlantic coast...adapting to the faster pace of life in a town while living and working in a busy port.

Martin suggested to Tom and his cousin Paddy that they should make the move and follow his example; repeating what they'd heard many times before. 'There's a good living to be made in England if you're prepared to work.'

'I've got plenty of work here, as you can see I've been converting this barn for sorting and packing eggs, one day when we're settled I'll take Nora to England, to Liverpool,' Tom said, smiling at the thought of taking Nora to visit her family in Liverpool.

'Nothing much changed at the quay, still the same for me loading and unloading ships all day, oh apart from more checks on the cargo for guns and stuff,' Paddy shrugged then added. 'How about a celebration jar or two in the bar down the road before I have to get back to work, Martin can tell us more about England.'

'Good idea, in any case they won't wont us here Mrs Murphy's friends are coming to help prepare food for the reception, there's nothing more to do we'd only be in the way,' Tom said with a wink to the others.

'A drink it is then,' Martin said picking up his coat.

Just as they were about to leave, the conversation was interrupted when Mrs Murphy and Nora appeared in the doorway of the cottage.

Surprised at seeing Tom's friend Nora inquired, 'Hello Martin when did you come home?' Before she could continue Mrs Murphy ignoring Nora's question, asked,

'Who are these two fine lads you've got helping you Tom?'

'Tom's friends Martin and his cousin Paddy, Martins' just over from England for the wedding, Nora explained, answering for Tom.

'Very nice boys you've done a good job you must be thirsty,' the old lady said.

'Would you like a drink?' Nora said looking at Tom as if he was the only one there.

'We're fine thanks Mrs Murphy, we're going into town,' Tom said looking a little sheepish.

'Be careful boys big day tomorrow, don't want to spoil it,' Mrs Murphy said warning the lads before they climbed onto the cart.

Chapter 54

The Wedding

Marry when June roses blow, over land and sea you'll go.

At the Murphy Farm on the night before the wedding, Nora's aunt recalled her own wedding day, telling her apprehensive and at the same time excited niece, what it was like getting married during the famine years when she was a young girl of twenty five.

'Nora darling, I know thing are bad for some with the evictions and all the poor folk leaving, like your da leaving to look for work in England. Do you know how lucky you are to have such a grand wedding? Your uncle and I couldn't afford to be wed in church, things were much worse then than they are now even with the evictions. There was some evictions, they were hardly needed people were dying of hunger every day. For folk wanting to wed before leaving the country a church wedding was out of the question, getting wed at home was the only option.

I was lucky working in the 'big house', that's how we survived the famine years.'

With Nora hanging onto every word on how weddings used to be her aunt went on to explain.

'The men-folk preferred home weddings, with no big church mass the feasting, drinking, and dancing could start sooner.

You're a lucky girl, you're marrying a lad with good prospects and you'll have a church wedding, you're a very lucky girl and he's a lucky lad, it's a good arrangement.

The only thing that bothered Nora was that her father had not yet arrived.

'Your father's cutting it fine if he's to walk you down the aisle tomorrow,' her aunt said looking through the window as if expecting him to see him walking towards the house.

'His letter said he'd be here today,' Nora replied anxiously.

'We'll see in the morning, best get some rest for the big day tomorrow,' Nora's aunt said easing herself out of her chair to prepare for bed.

It was very likely that word had got to the Militia, that a big wedding would take place in town and their men would be posted in the in the town watching the celebrations.

Father Quinn took Tom and his brother Mick aside after at the last meeting of the Ballingar branch of the Land League to suggest that league members could help on the day of the wedding.

'Our man Samuel Daley will be there with the Militia outside the church keeping watch for potential trouble. Members of our Castlebar branch will be placed along the route to the church. 'We want the wedding of one of our members to go smoothly and without any trouble that's why we'll have our men there.'

The wedding day Sunday June 1st 1879.

An hour before the wedding ceremony was due to start Father Byrne instructed his senior alter-boy to light the candles, then he set about checking the rest of the church to see that all was in order before the first guests arrived. Friends of Nora's aunt had been busy decorating the central aisle and doorway with garlands of flowers filling the air with a pleasing aroma brightening the dimly lit interior.

Father Byrne wasn't surprised by the large crowd gathered outside the church, it was to be expected. Word had got around the county and beyond of the wedding of Thomas Walsh the youngest son of one of the county's foremost businessmen. The wedding had been announced at morning mass on the previous four weeks from the pulpits of Westport, Castlebar and Ballingar churches as well as talked about at the local markets.

Two days before the wedding, Tom's brother Mick had been busy adapting the most suitable cart in their yard to transport Nora to church by fitting a raised seat. His sister Maria finished the job by garlanding it with flowers while his father Joe groomed two of the best ponies on the farm until their silky smooth coats were shining in the summer sun.

Nora travelled to the church from the Murphy farm on the garlanded cart with her auntie sitting next to Mick Fox. (Mick had offered to drive the cart when the wedding was announced at the last Land League meeting). As brides do Nora looked radiant sitting under an arch of pink and white wild roses with her red hair flowing in curls down her back. Wearing the wedding gown and veil that was given to her aunt twenty five years earlier for her wedding by Lady Boyle her employer at the 'big house', made the 'radiant bride' look complete. In train bridesmaid Maria, on a similarly decorated cart driven by Land League member John Mulloy.

By the time the bridal carts were nearing the church they had been joined by other invited guests, some walking others riding on various modes of transport making an entertaining spectacle for the townsfolk gathered in front to the church.

'Welcome to my church Nora Murphy, before we begin the service there's someone here to see you,' Father Byrne greeted the bride as Mick Fox helped her alight from the cart. Before Nora could ask why anyone would want to see her just before her wedding a man stepped out into the daylight from behind the church door. It was the man she had hoped would be there to walk her down the aisle, her father.

Nora picked up her dress and ran to his arms,

'Da, da, you made it, I missed you and ma,' after a long embrace, 'you can meet my Tommy after the service.'

'Make it brief you can talk later.' Father Byrne said softly looking at his pocket watch.

Introductions over, father, bride and her bridesmaid prepared to walk down the aisle to join her husband to be at the altar.

Waiting by the altar next to Martin, his best man and best friend, Tom's head filled with thoughts of the last six months from collecting and delivering eggs in an area covering most of North Mayo, to waiting in the church to be married.

The day he meet Nora, a young girl he saw walking down the hill to the bakery, swinging her basket as if she hadn't a care in the world.

Taking Martin his best friend to Westport to look for work in England. Witnessing a cruel eviction on the way.

Joining the Land League to help stop the injustices inflicted on the poor cottiers.

Seeing a false vision on Knockmore church wall.

Wrongly arrested for a raid on the 'big house' and imprisoned in the Castlebar Barracks.

Yes it's been quite a journey Tom thought up as the organ music signalled the start of the wedding ceremony.

The End

Printed in Great Britain
by Amazon

41561629R00090